Wings Upon Flames

Sean Malloy

Published by Sean Malloy, 2019.

This is a work of fiction. Similarities to real people, places, or events are entirely coincidental.

WINGS UPON FLAMES

First edition. October 18, 2019.

Written by Sean Malloy.

Wings
Upon
Flames

Wings
Upon
Flames

SHORT STORIES

SEAN MALLOY

For Rebecka, Ben, Nickolas, and Juliette.
Your love gives me confidence and determination.

For Mom, and Dad, and Kristen.
Your love and support fueled my passions and interests.

Wings Upon Flames

THE WINGS OF THE GARGANTUAN creature expanded over fifty feet wide, the veiny skin thinly spread across a sturdy boned structure like the membrane of a large bat wing. Its skin was like thick scaled armor, rough as stone. Even the sharpest steel tip arrows could not pierce this demon's armor. We would need something much bigger to take this monster down.

The eyes splayed open to an amber-engorged, black-diamond sliver. It watched me as I stood there, staring at me with a cautionary wonderment. I gazed back at the beautiful creature seeing my reflection in its glassy eyes. It snorted like it could smell the fear exuding from my pores. The claws were the size of my body, scraping the solid stone wall of the tower like it were a jaguar climbing a tree. If it decided to eat me, I would be the easiest prey it had ever encountered.

The fire consumed the homes below, the homes of the poor and the weak on the outer limits of the castle walls. The sticks and straw that were used to keep the elements from inside their walls were now ablaze because the demon from the sky came to prove it was more powerful than us humans. The warming, orange embers soared into the night sky, heavily glowing and illuminating the glossy, tar-colored skin and the violet belly of the beast. Its snakelike tongue flicked out of its mouth with a faint sound of a hiss. I was frozen in amazement, still with fear. The cries of the injured coming from down below woke me from my trance. Its extensive tail nestled close to its hind legs and the majestic head of the beast bowed down as I reached my hand out, inching closer to its nostrils. I could see the sense of hesitation in its eyes, the diamond iris judging me, sharpening to a sliver as I held my hand closer to the beast. My fingertips felt the rocky surface of its scales and its iris flooded open like water flowing out of a broken dam. Its nose pushed my hand and the weight of my body effortlessly, inching me backward. My mind lit with pure ecstasy as my hand grazed the ginormous beast's face, along its jaw and under the eye that watched my every movement. *How could such a destructive beast be so kind and humble? Why was it here and where did it come from?* I had heard stories of dragons as a young lad, but never did I meet one, see one, nor known anyone who had seen one before. The night sky was lit from the fire among black clouds of smoke. I continued to slide my hand down its neck to the torso, sliding my feet alongside its appendages that could pulverize me in a single swipe. Seconds before it took off like a bird in flight, my wife called to me from below where my attention had been diverted. I turned back around to see the majestic creature, but it was gone. It had taken off stealthily like it was never here at all. The damage was done, people were hurt badly, some were caught in the flames and burned to death. I hunted the beast for years after, I waited for the creature's return, but I never saw the gigantic wings span these castle walls again.

Life Stream

JAKE JUMPED OUT OF the water. The smell of summer filled the air, honeysuckle and cut grass with a drop of gasoline. The sun dipped below the horizon which made the sky look like a rainbow lollipop. Clouds like cotton candy dissolved into the atmosphere like they were being swallowed by the stars above. The chlorine stung his eyes from peeking underwater where the world looked so different. Sometimes the silence soothed him, to the point where he wished he had gills so he could breathe like a fish.

The plastic rungs of the ladder gripped under Jake's wet feet while holding onto the arched metal connecting both sides of the above-ground pool. Jake always welcomed a challenge to jump from high places as he plunged to the ground from the third rung down, rolled onto his back, and laid in the soft, springy grass that tickled his bare skin and made him itchy. Jake's blue eyes wandered off to the stars in wonderment of what they were, and how he could get there. His dreams were disrupted by loud yelling from inside the house.

Jake's father, Robert, must have been drunk again because his speech grew in anger, and in volume with every passing second. His mother, Tonia, sounded like she was pleading with

Robert, trying her best to reason with him—to keep him calm. Her high-pitched voice shook behind the screen door that separated the world from war and peace. Jake leapt to his feet from sheer moments of relaxation lying in prickly grass, his heart jolting his nervous system to high tension.

Jake was too young to understand what caused Robert's rage, but he knew it had to do with the drinking. The funny scent that permeated from Robert's pores helped Jake know when to hide away somewhere invisible to Robert, until he was no longer conscious to make any decisions. It was like a demon possessed him anytime the liquor funneled into his bloodstream. He went from a decent human being, supporting a family and a house on a government paycheck, which wasn't much, to inflicting physical and emotion damage on both Tonia and Jake.

Jake remembered a day when Robert didn't smell of alcohol for a long time. The police force liked Robert because he was a good officer, but they needed him to be clean on the job, didn't matter what he did after he left the precinct. After a few months, Robert left A.A. and went back to the same old habits. Go to work, come home, drink, beat Tonia, beat Jake, pass out, and do it again tomorrow.

The sliding glass door opened to the deck of his one-story house, the aluminum siding with dings in it from Jake and his friends playing baseball out in the backyard. Robert made sure Jake received the appropriate punishment for doing such an atrocious thing to the house he owned.

Robert stepped outside. Tonia's cries echoed through the kitchen and out the open door where the neighbors would call the police if they knew the police would help. As a Suffolk

County police officer in Brentwood, he dealt with *the scum of the earth as* he would always say. Jake thought, *"Was it the same kind of scum that hits their wife and kid?"*

Robert had a permanent look of disdain plastered to his lips and a slight stagger in his walk. He came outside to give Jake some trouble and Jake wanted none of it.

"Get ova 'ere boy." Robert always called Jake boy. He could only remember his father calling him by his name twice in his life, and both times Robert had been in A.A. and off the booze for longer than a week.

Jake hesitated to move toward the beast.

"Did ya 'ear me?" Robert stared at Jake with a stern, irritated look.

"You leave him alone," Tonia yelled from inside the house with a hysterical weep.

Jake gulped hard and walked up the steps of the deck, looking his father in the eyes. If Jake didn't make eye contact with Robert, he would get smacked for disrespect. This is something that he learned after a few times of receiving heavy hands and red cheeks.

"It's time for dinner. You get in there and eat what yo' momma made or I'm gonna find that belt dat you like so much." Jakes eyes widened. As he ran inside, his swim trunks were damp from the pool and the bottom of the trucks dripped a small stream down his leg.

His mother hovered over the stove scraping the pan of burnt biscuits with a spatula and using an oven mitt to hold the high-tempered metal. Tonia wore a red handprint across her cheek, and tears trickled to her chin. She was dressed in faded jeans, a jewel sequined, turquoise t-shirt, and white *Keds, all* topped with puffy hair pulled back in a scrunchy. She snif-fled and held back her cries in front of Jake while managing to scrape each biscuit from the tray. Tonia diffused most situ-ations that could've led to bad beatings for Jake by taking the brunt of Robert's abusive behavior.

Jake sat at the table in between his father and his mother. The plate was filled with overdone steak, broccoli, and burnt biscuits. Robert sat down in the head chair of the table and scooted in, hovering over his plate of food. He cut through the tough steak with a sharp knife. The sawing motion wobbled the table, spilling some water out of the glasses and rattling the forks and glass plates. The tough meat needed to be doused in A1 steak sauce to salvage any taste. Robert chewed the meat with a look of contempt toward Tonia. His hands sprawled out on the table with fork and knife angled toward the ceiling. The summer air crept in through the screens of the open windows, a cool breeze that reminded Jake that he wasn't wearing a shirt.

"Can I be excused from the table, Dad?" Jake said, rubbing his bare shoulders.

Robert looked at him, placed his utensils down on the plaid tablecloth, and nodded while he continued to chew the rubbery meat. Jake ejected himself from the seat and ran across the linoleum kitchen floor, down the soft brown carpet of the hallway to his room where he closed the door and rummaged through his drawer for a t-shirt and a pair of dry shorts. Any moment Jake could escape his father would be moments he reveled in freedom—even if it was for just a few minutes.

JAKE AWOKE IN HIS BED a sweaty mess; the cries of his mother woke him like he was still living in the same house. The smacking sound of his father's hand hitting his mother haunted him in his sleep. Jake's heart raced, and his chest filled with anger and anxiety. Up until the moment he sprung from the covers of his bed, he heard Robert reprimanding Tonia while she wept in pain. No matter how many times he went to a therapist, or how good things were going in his life, he would relive this nightmare, and no one did anything to help because Jake lived in a neighborhood of cowards. Jake remembered the one time a neighbor reported a fight Robert and Tonia had at two in the morning. The next day Robert went to Mr. Robinson's house, clubbed the mailbox off the post with his nightstick, and threw it on the roof of Mr. Robinson's house. When Mr. Robinson came outside, fear filled his eyes as Robert pointed his nightstick at him and said, "If you report me again it will be your head on the roof, not the mailbox." So, the neighborhood shut their eyes and covered their ears whenever Robert beat his wife and child.

JAKE SAT AT THE SIDE of his father's hospital bed. He remembered the way that he treated him as a child. He wanted to tell his father that he hated him, that he was the reason for his mother's untimely death years ago. But he didn't. He sat there in an uncomfortable plastic chair, little more than a thin, mesh-covered cushion and uncooperative plastic arms. Jake leaned over, held his head in his hands, as the hate filled his heart. There was at least a small level of satisfaction he received knowing that his father was dying a slow death from cirrhosis of the liver. Robert's yellowed skin and white stubbled hair looked mangled and old. His upper torso was propped up from the mechanical bed and the plain white blanket covered him from his waist to his feet. A cough came from behind the curtain from the other patient in the room. Jake split the lids of his eyes apart, angled up to the corner of the room where a game show played out on the TV. Somewhere deep inside Jake felt this obligation to be here, to watch his father pass away, mainly for closure if nothing else.

Jake remembered his mother's face the day before she died. Her tired wrinkles under her eyes, the beaming glow of her smile as Jake walked into the room. All her worries went away when she looked into his innocent eyes. Jake was fifteen when Tonia passed, and Jake blamed Robert for her death. Although Robert didn't kill her, she was taken to the Lord that night because of his drunken, abusive behavior. Why she stayed with him was beyond Jake's understanding.

The hospital room smelled of chicken noodle soup, triggering a fond memory linked to cold afternoons inside with his mother. The scent became nauseating after a few minutes, curdling the blood beneath the surface of Jake's skin. Robert's EKG machine persisted to beep infuriating Jake like the sound of jackhammer. Each beep pulverized his ear drum and dented his fragile heart.

Jake last talked to his father about five years ago. It had been the moment where he finally stood up to Robert and voiced his opinion about how he felt as a child.

"Mom and I were terrified of you. You were a ticking time bomb, waiting to explode."

"You think I had it easy? My job and the people I dealt with daily was enough to drive anyone mad."

"So why were you the only one to abuse his family then?" Jake said. The anger filled his chest like a balloon. "It wasn't the job, Dad. It was the drinking. Mom and I didn't deserve the horror show you became."

"You don't know what you're talking about boy."

"I know that you were a self-loathing piece of shit excuse for a human being."

"You better watch your tone with me boy or I'll..."

"Or you'll what?" Jake said, inching himself closer to his father's face, staring him right in the eyes just as he was taught. "Hit me?" Robert stood there silent. "That's what I thought. Nothing." Jake turned and walked away.

"You know if it wasn't for me you wouldn't be the man you are today," Robert said as Jake retreated from him.

"That's a sorry excuse for bad parenting, Dad. And after mom died, you were even worse because you didn't care about me at all." Jake said, cocking his head over his shoulder.

"Sounds like you whine a lot, just like your mother."

"You don't talk about my mother that way." Jake stomped back toward Robert. "You're half the person she could ever be, and if anyone was supposed to die in that car crash it should have been you, but you were too drunk like always. She died to get fucking milk because you couldn't stay sober for one day." Jake held his finger in Robert's face.

"Hey, I told her not to go out in that weather, she didn't listen to me like usual."

"There is no reasoning with you while you are like this." Jake slammed his hands at his sides. "You never did anything wrong," Jake said sarcastically while he walked away again.

"I miss your mother, too."

"You miss her because she took care of your drunken ass," Jake shouted behind him.

"She took care of you, too."

"Go fuck yourself. I don't even know why I come over here, hoping one day you will change. After mom died, I thought you would transform into something better, but you didn't. You didn't even shed a tear at her funeral." Jake stood by his car outside the front of Robert's house.

"I don't cry like a sissy boy. That's your job apparently."

Jake got in his car and sped off down the block, leaving his father standing there with a drunken grin.

JAKE WORKED AT THE airport where he started off as luggage assistant and then worked his way to assistant manager of operations, communicating with pilots about federal regulations, training new employees, and working closely with the manager to prepare financial reports and maintain airport records. He built his life around his work and kept his family drama out of his mind while he advanced his career. In the five years he hadn't spoken to his father, Jake rose to a good paying job that he enjoyed being around, helping customers to keep his mind busy. It was the day he received a call about his father that reminded him of his childhood. It was like the summer breeze warmed his face once more. How could something so pleasant, remind him of such terrible times? Although he didn't want to see his father, he felt he must, to start the grieving process.

The whole ride to the hospital, he thought about his mother. Jake smiled. Big plastic curlers and a blow dryer turned her amber colored hair into thick curls bouncing with every step. A floral scent drifted around the house whenever Tonia brought home gardenias resting on the windowsill of the kitchen. Her gigantic laugh made him smile every time he heard it, even while he watched cartoons on the tube set television with the bunny ears spread high into the corners of the living room ceiling.

He remembered her tickle fights she started where they both ended up on the floor giggling uncontrollably until they couldn't breathe. Gasping for air, they'd lie face up on the warm, fluffy carpet in his bedroom—following the blades of his ceiling fan, Jake's eyeballs circled around in their sockets as fast as they could, so he saw one singular blade go around and around. He would do this until he got dizzy and felt like his eyeballs were going to roll right out of his head.

The white beams of light that flashed over the asphalt, yellow lines disappeared under his tires as he drifted out of his lane, correcting his wheel and car horns honking from oncoming traffic woke him from his euphoric memory.

Jake pulled up to the hospital and parked his car outside the monstrous building. The bluish hue from the fluorescent flood lights and the multitude of windows lit from the inside looked like a checkerboard lying on its side. The pattern was almost symmetrical and intentionally lit in a cadence. Jake hated hospitals. The last time he was at this hospital his mother was here on her deathbed. His neck bent, he lit a cigarette and took a drag leaning up against the hood of his 2007 Acura RSX. The vehicle had over 100,000 miles on it, but it still ran well.

Jake walked through the halls of the hospital. He passed an endless amount of rooms with identical, large, wooden doors. Grey walls, slightly greenish from the flicker of the overhead fluorescent lights stretched down the hallway in a pattern dividing lines like a highway on the ceiling.

Jake finally walked through one door and saw his sick father asleep, propped up in a mechanical bed. A nurse came in to check on his father and saw Jake there.

"Oh, I'm sorry, I didn't know you were in here."

"It's ok. I didn't mean to startle you."

"I'll come back in a few minutes and give you some time with him."

"No, that's ok. Do what you have to. I can stand over here and wait."

"It's no problem, I'm just changing his dressing. I can come back later."

"I insist. It's really no problem. We didn't really have the best relationship anyways. Not sure why I'm telling you that."

"I see," she said. "I'm sorry to hear that. I didn't even know who my father was if that helps you feel any better."

"Sorry." Jake wanted to say more but stopped there. He watched the nurse change Robert's I.V. bag and administer a morphine drip to ease his pain. She was so careful and gentle. He couldn't help peeking at her backside as she bent over his father to pull his covers down. He looked back up at her. Her black hair was pulled back into a ponytail and even without makeup she was a pretty girl. He could tell she was a runner because she had a slim frame and thick legs. Her toned arms looked like she barely had an ounce of fat on her. He shook his head and tried to come up with something interesting to say.

"So, how long have you been working here?" He cleared his throat and scratched the back of his neck, diverting his eyes to the floor.

"About five years."

"You like it?"

"Yeah. You going to ask any other obvious questions?" she said sarcastically and laughed. Jake chuckled.

"Sorry, just don't know what to say I guess."

"You don't have to. Most family of patients try talking to me about things because they think they're being polite, but it's just more awkward when they talk while I'm working."

"Well you're pretty honest."

"I try to be."

"That's a good policy to have I guess."

"Listen if you want to talk more about anything, I'll be downstairs in a half hour for my coffee break. You can meet me down there and we can talk about other things or nothing if you want."

"Oh... Ok...Sure," Jake's heart skipped a beat. He didn't know if she asked him downstairs for a date or just to have someone to talk with.

"Alright. See you then." She pulled off her latex gloves and threw them into the trash can as she walked out to the hall.

Jake watched his father in the hospital bed for five minutes after the nurse had left. The tubes in his father's nose that provided oxygen looked like long strands of spaghetti connected to a machine that looked like something out of the Millennium Falcon. Robert was breathing regularly and seemed to be fine.

Sitting so close to his father made Jake feel like he should leave the room. He should go downstairs to meet with the nurse. He didn't want to stand her up if this was considered a date in some circumstances, but he didn't want to seem urgent either, or desperate, so he killed time waiting for the clock to hit the top of the hour. Jake nervously tapped the arm of the chair with his fingernails, a habit his father always hated. Robert used to scream at him for tapping on everything and anything Jake's little hands encountered. It was a nervous tick that took years of beatings to stop. Since he'd been living on his own the impulse came back. The clock hit 9 p.m. and Jake got out of his seat and stretched his shirt trying to get the wrinkles out.

He made his way downstairs after he sat next to his father, listening to his mechanical breathing, and a constant beep that rang in his ears. The sound ticked in his brain like it was a metronome while he stood on the elevator surrounded by shiny titanium walls. His flesh colored reflection blurred around him. When the elevator reached level, the sliding doors opened to waxed terrazzo floors. A few patients in wheelchairs were pushed by nurses down the hallway. With his hands in his pockets, Jake entered the cafeteria. The nurse was sitting at a table in the corner of the room by herself with a tray of food. She saw him walk through the doorway and waved him over.

"Hey, I'm sorry, I don't believe I got your name before," Jake said, pulling his hands from his pockets.

"Stephanie, but everyone around here calls me Steph." Steph stood up and reached her hand out to Jake.

"Nice to meet you officially Stephanie, or Steph I should say."

"Nice to meet you..." They shook hands and Steph looked at Jake with her eyebrows raised in question.

"Oh, sorry. Jake. My name's Jake." He shook her hand awkwardly faster.

"Thanks, Jake." She took her hand and wiped it on her scrubs.

"Sorry. I just had my hands in my pockets."

"It's ok, just take a seat." Steph sat down, and Jake inched a chair out from the table, the legs shrieked made them cringe just a little. Jake sat down and looked at Steph while she forked some Caesar salad into her mouth while lifting her phone from the table to check her notifications.

There was awkward silence followed by loud yelling back and forth by two janitors verbally fighting in Spanish. One held up an empty jug of bleach and spewed some words fast and loud. It was hard for anyone to understand what he was saying.

"What was that?" Jake asked Steph.

"I don't know. Those two are always at it," Steph said with a mouthful of salad. She wiped her mouth with a napkin as she chewed on the leafy greens smothered in creamy Caesar dressing. "What's with you and your dad?" she said, swallowing her last mouthful.

"He was a cop when I was a kid till he got kicked off the force for intoxication while on patrol."

"Well that's a good way to get kicked out of the academy."

"Yeah, sometimes I think he took it out on my mom and me. One of the reasons why my mom..." Jake stopped and looked away from Steph.

"What happened with your mom?" She leaned in closer to Jake. "It's ok, you can tell me."

"She died. Because of his habits."

"I'm sorry to hear that."

"Nothing to be sorry about. It wasn't your fault," Jake said sarcastically.

"Listen I didn't mean to pry but you kind of left me hanging. And I am sorry about your mom. No young boy should lose his mother." Steph planted her hand on top of his hand resting on the table. They locked eyes for a moment and Jake sniffed as he was fighting with his allergies.

"How's the food here?" Jake asked, pulling his hand out from under Steph's.

"It's alright. It's hospital food so, I would give it a B on the best day. Usually that is Taco Tuesday. For some strange reason they have great tacos here, but everything else is mediocre at best."

"I think I'm going to grab something to eat. Anything to stay away from up there."

"Do not get the salmon."

"Got it." Jake got up and went into the cafeteria's kitchen where there was food under stainless steel covered trays. He opened a lid and saw some old looking, stuffed shells with dried out sauce. Popped the lid to another to find stiff chicken cutlets as if they were preparing jerky. He opened another lid and the salmon was in this one. The pinkish color was almost brown, and it smelled just as bad as it looked. He threw the lid back on and walked over to the refrigerated coolers with salads, pudding, and sandwiches stacked on each shelf. He grabbed the Caesar salad since Steph was eating it, so it couldn't be that bad. He grabbed the salad dressing packets in a bucket at the bottom of the cooler, then a fork next to the refrigerator on the top of a cabinet with all the dining utensils, next to some condiments in a metal box stuffed in cylindrical holes.

Jake walked over to the register and the attendant scanned his food without saying a word to him.

"Card or cash?" she said with her earbuds still in.

"Card," he said back, looking at her long and disappointed face. She looked bored out of her mind.

"Insert the chip," she mumbled.

Jake inserted the card and it beeped and told him: *Card error, please try again.*

"Not yet."

"When?"

"Now."

"Now?"

"Now." He inserted the card again and it read back: *Card error, please try again.*

"What's going on?" he said heatedly.

"You did it wrong."

"Which other way is there to insert the damn chip?"

"You did it too soon."

"This isn't my first time entering a chip into a machine." Fury raised in his voice. He was about to yell at the girl when Steph came up to him.

"Hey, Doris. I got this one, ok?"

"Alright, Steph," Doris said with a smile. Jake looked over at Steph, insulted and embarrassed at the same time.

"Don't worry, it's my treat."

"I didn't need you to do that," he said, placing his card in his wallet.

Steph inserted her card and the payment went through. Doris handed over a receipt after it buzzed out of the small printer.

"I could see you were getting frustrated there."

"She was egging me on."

"Doris is Doris," she said and laughed. "So, I see you took my advice and didn't get the salmon, but you got exactly what I have."

"I figured it was the only safe choice."

"Usually the salad isn't. But it looked fresh today."

"Well thanks for telling me."

"No problem." Steph laughed. "You need to lighten up, you know that?"

"I'm just stressed from being here, I guess. I haven't seen my dad in five years and it's bringing back all these emotions from the last time I saw him."

"I get that. I do. But just try to chill a bit and just have a conversation with me without trying to blow a gasket in that head of yours."

"I'll try." Jake wanted to explode on Steph. She didn't know him—she didn't know what he went through with his father. He stepped back from his negative thoughts for a moment and realized that she probably saw this kind of thing daily.

"So, what happened with your father?"

"He was killed in Afghanistan."

"I'm sorry."

"What are you sorry for, you didn't do anything," Steph said sarcastically. Her brown eyes blinked at him rapidly. Jake chuckled. "Now you know how that feels," she said, looking away from him.

"Was your father in the war?"

"Yeah. He was in the Navy SEALs. That's all I really know."

"He must have been a bad ass then."

"Probably. The only thing I have of him are pictures while he was with my mom before he was deployed. He died before I was born here in this hospital."

"That must've been rough to grow up without a father."

"It was. My mother was scarred by it pretty badly, so I basically raised myself."

"Sounds like we both have bad family situations."

"We both lost someone, and it affected the rest of our lives. But life goes on," Steph said, wiping a tear from her eye."

"I didn't mean to make you cry."

"You didn't. It's nothing really. Just bad memories."

"I feel that way all the time," Jake said and reached his hand across the table and gently placed his fingers over Steph's hand. His palm rested on her fingers while they shared glances. The silence between the two of them was powerful. It was like they could feel each other's pain for a moment. Their upbringing was tough, but they got through it and were successful in their careers.

"It's amazing how we turned out even in those circumstances."

"Well I'm sure we're messed up in some way, shape, or form."

"Speak for yourself," Steph said and laughed. Jake chuckled back.

"My lunch break is almost over." Steph glanced at her watch.

"Oh...Ok."

"This was fun. Maybe we can do it again tomorrow if you are around?"

"I would like that."

Steph got up from the table and grabbed her tray. She looked at Jake again, smiled, and walked away to the garbage cans where she emptied the trash and placed the tray above the swinging door of the trash bin.

Jake opened the salad container, ripped the tear line and squeezed the creamy dressing all over the green leaves and croutons. He picked up his black plastic fork and mixed the salad around. He stabbed at the lettuce and forked it into his mouth. Chewing on the crispy greens and the crunchy croutons, he noticed he was missing a drink. He slapped his head, not wanting to deal with Doris again.

OVER THE NEXT FEW DAYS, Jake visited Robert at the hospital, but found the main reason he was there was to see Steph. She wasn't like any other girl he ever met before. Steph wasn't the spoiled, daddy's girl he was used to dating. Jake was comforted by her family drama that was as messed up as his, if not worse. They both commiserated together, lifting the weight of the heavy burdens they carried through most of their lives.

Jake felt like he finally met someone that got him, understood him enough to have a conversation that was refreshing and new. The other girls he dated didn't compare to Steph; good looking girls, but they didn't seem to have the same fire that burned inside of her. There was something about her eyes that were like nothing he'd ever seen before. There was life and purpose, even though her spirit had been broken just like his, there was clarity and focus–drive and ambition. Jake had an obstinate feeling that he should be more morose with Robert being in a coma he probably wouldn't wake from, but, for the first time in a long time, he was happy.

Jake came to the hospital after eight o'clock like he normally did, but this time he got out of his vehicle with a rose in hand. He was jittery, licking his lips uncontrollably. He didn't know how Steph would take this, if she would go out with him, if she would see him outside of the hospital. Jake knew that Steph started rounds of patients in his father's wing after visiting hours were over. With hopes of surprising Steph, Jake planned to get to Robert's room before she got there.

He got off the elevator and walked down the hall to Robert's room. He turned the corner into his father's room, but he wasn't there. The bed was empty, and it was stripped clean. The machines were turned off, black screens stared back at him. Confused, Jake checked the room number. He popped his head around the corner of the door, a plastic plaque with the number 809A hung from the wall. This was his father's room. Jake squeezed the rose tightly, forgetting it was in his hand, and forgetting that it still had a few thorns on it. The thorn pierced his finger, and he dropped the rose and let out an unnerving moan. Blood trickled from his index finger. He examined it and sucked the metallic taste from his finger. He bent over and picked up the rose when Steph came around the corner and saw him standing there.

"Jake!" she yelled out down the hall. She ran towards him.

"Where's my father, Steph?"

"He's in surgery right now. He went into cardiac arrest. They are doing what they can right now."

"Can you bring me to him?" For some strange reason he felt bad for his father and he wanted to be there for him. He knew it was against his instincts, but he wanted to see him.

"Yeah, follow me." She turned and walked fast. She cocked her head behind her. "Who's the rose for?"

Trying to catch up, Jake skipped every few steps to match Steph's speed.

"It's for you," he said, out of breath.

"What for?" She continued forward to the elevator and pressed the button that lit up yellow. The red digital screen above the elevator doors climbed in number from the ground floor up. Jake caught his breath and focused on the situation. He awkwardly handed her the rose and continued to suck on his finger. He wiped his saliva-soaked finger on the back of his shirt.

"I wasn't expecting this to be like... this," he said with a deep exhale.

"What do you mean?" Steph said, holding the rose in between her index finger and her thumb, simultaneously sniffing it like it was the natural thing to do when handed a flower.

"I didn't expect my dad to be having surgery. I just wanted to come up here and tell you that I liked spending time with you." They walked onto the elevator.

"That is nice. I like spending time with you too."

"Maybe we could go to dinner sometime." Their eyes met but something didn't seem right with Steph. She held something back as the doors closed.

"Maybe we can talk about it later. Let's go see your dad." Steph darted out of the elevator when the doors opened. Jake followed her as she cut some corners down a wing and through double doors that led them to a room with a glass window. He looked in on Robert being operated on by a team of surgeons. Steph stood next to Jake for a moment and held onto his arm as he stared through the glass, ghostly pale like the life was sucked out of him. This all reminded him too much of his mother and how she died. The pain that man had put him through. Jake felt his heart sink to his stomach and resurface as he remembered to breathe. It was like he rode a rollercoaster that dropped one hundred feet and was over in a few seconds. Almost choking on his own saliva, he backed away from the window.

"Are you ok?" Steph said calmly.

"No. I need to sit down."

"Let's get you to the waiting room." Steph pulled his arm and he reluctantly followed like his feet were glued to the floor. The image of his father's chest pried open couldn't be deleted. It was hard to turn away, but his stomach felt like he had food poisoning suddenly.

Steph pulled him out and walked him into the waiting room with about fifteen empty chairs and a stack of magazines strewn about on an end table against the wall. Steph sat him down.

"Want some water?" she said, but Jake only heard muffled sounds. He just nodded his head yes and a moment later she filled his hand with a paper cup filled with some ice-cold water. Steph sat next to Jake while he thought about the times when he was little, the ones he could remember that he spent with his father, maybe a good time.

Jake remembered the time that they went on the father-son fishing trip, but his father was completely piss drunk. He was so drunk that one of the other fathers on the boat said something to him about being belligerent and Robert punched him in the face. They had to end the boat trip early because of it, and he never went fishing with his father again after that.

Jake tried to imagine it like Robert was the father he always wanted. The one that went fishing with him and taught him how to fish.

Little Jake stood there against the railing and held his fishing pole in the air, his hook dangling about.

"How do I hook the bait, Dad?"

"I'll show you." Robert took the bait in his hand, its little fish head with its dead eyes ogled at Jake and nothing at the same time. His father put the head in between his index and thumb and pushed the hook through with his other hand right below the eyes. The hook pierced through and Robert swung the body of the fish and let it dangle there.

"Did you see that?"

"Yeah. That was gross."

"It's the only way to catch a bigger fish Jakey."

"Big fish eat smaller fish?"

"Yeah, they do. And big fish are eaten by even bigger fish, sometimes even sharks."

"Sharks!" Jake excitedly jumped with joy. "Are we going to catch a shark?"

"Maybe, Buddy."

"Maybe a big fish will eat this small fish and then the big fish will get eaten by the shark, and then I can meet a real live shark." A level of excitement electrified through young Jake's voice. Robert laughed and continued to bait his own hook.

"Now we have to cast the line. Watch me." Robert flicked his wrist and the hooked bait flew through the air and into the brownish water. "Now you try."

Jake swung the pole but forgot to hold the casting reel down, so the bait swung back around and caught itself on the railing of the boat, flinging the bait into the water. Jake let out a moan.

"I guess the fish get that one for free today." Robert chuckled.

Little Jake smiled back at Robert and hugged the side of his leg. He enjoyed this memory even if it was made up. Maybe this was the way he was meant to look back on his childhood. It was a way to let go of his father, the way he was brought up by making completely new memories, ones that didn't happen at all.

As he sat there in the waiting room with Steph sitting next to him, he smiled and felt the settling of his stomach. His heartrate slowed, and a blanket of calmness covered him and, for the first time in his life, he felt there was peace surrounding him. The burden of his childhood died in that room, and his problems were lifted off his shoulders. The feeling left him weightless for the first time like he was actually floating underwater.

The Audition

"You only get one shot, do not miss your chance to blow.
This opportunity comes once in a lifetime."
-Eminem

ACT ONE

EVIL COMES IN ALL SHAPES and sizes just like the good. When I was a young girl, no one told me that I would encounter evil face to face when I least expected it. We all believe that these things happen to other people, but never to ourselves. I could have done things differently, but it can't be undone now. I encountered an evil that claimed my unborn son's life when I was only eighteen years old. The tragedy left me within inches of life myself but took the innocence of a person that had done no wrong. I was devastated. Changed forever. Most people didn't know of my horrific encounter because I told no one about my pregnancy to begin with. I had just graduated high school and about to continue my education in drama school at USC.

I didn't go to acting school. I did nothing for a while. A career I wanted so bad had been thrown away in seconds. Years of going to acting workshops, booking commercials, building a reel for college all went away in a snap. Eight years went by and at twenty-six I had enough of feeling sorry for myself. It was time to pursue my passion in life, not because I could, but because I needed to dedicate my life to my little boy that I never got to enjoy. I imagined what his face would look like at this moment. The smiles and the giggles that would have been instilled in my memory forever were only dreams. I did it for him. I pushed myself for him. I failed for him, with hopes to succeed and see his smiling face one day when we meet on the other side.

FADE-IN TO A LONELY girl sitting in a white plastic chair. We pull out to see her nestled against a puke green wall—covered in posters from films this company had cast before. There is a room full of women ranging from late teens to early thirties, sitting in a row on either side of this small overcrowded room. Pretty faces stand along the empty space by the entrance, awkwardly, and uncomfortably.

That's me, Sara Mackenzie, the lonely girl in the cinematic slow pull from a close-up to a wide establishing shot in a casting lobby. Sometimes I imagine my life will be told as a film one day, but until then I just dream it. This isn't my first audition, although I can see that some of these girls are probably popping their cherries today, figuratively speaking in auditioning terms that is. Some of them are hopeful and young and haven't experienced the let downs of the business yet. Some other girls, like the one sitting across from me, have had to use their talents for manipulating directors to get the roles that they want. Jenna

Gold, her stage name–her real name is Jennifer Goldstein, is a beautiful blonde with big boobs and an IMDB page most girls would kill for. Fortunately for me, I haven't had to put out that way to get a role.

I work as a bartender at the neighborhood Ruby Tuesday to support my acting habits. Acting workshops four nights a week, go to work after classes, wake up in the morning and go to auditions hoping to land some parts on television and in some indie films.

The success I had in commercials had people recognizing me on the street as that girl I played in a commercial for prescription medication for herpes. The small roles I've had on TV and in films render me still; that girl that no one knows, not pretty enough to get a lead role, and not dorky enough to be the recurring role like Abby Sciuto on a show like NCIS.

This is what is happening now. I'm waiting here with my headphones in my ears listening to *Troublemaker* by Beach House. The dreamy guitar riffs and melodic vocals lets me focus so I can access a part of me that I'll use for the character I am auditioning for.

I'm what they call a character actor and I take them home with me all the time. I am transformed when I access these other personalities and it has caused me to lose some friends, jobs, and forced me to alienate my parents from time to time. But this is what I do to play the game. It is like tennis, bouncing the ball back and forth with your opponent until the game is over.

"Jenna Gold," Diane the casting assistant shouted without even looking up from her clipboard. Her graying hair pinned in a bun reflected the lack of makeup she was wearing and was further accented by a black shawl over a white camisole. Diane was too young to have gray hair, but her face told how tired she was from the long hours of casting—probably at least twelve different characters to put on tape for the director and producers today.

Jenna stood up, adjusted her boobs, and flung her platinum blonde hair over her shoulders. She walked through the doorway, slightly pulling down her mini skirt to show off her toned abs and to hide just enough of her nether regions to keep the men's imagination running wild. Almost every time I've been on an audition with her, she got the part, and I can't imagine why. *Insert sarcasm.* But Hollywood is changing these days with this hashtag me too stuff going on. I'm surprised she hasn't come forward with anything yet, but I'm sure that would hurt her reputation for roles she clearly didn't deserve. *Insert sarcasm again.* Sorry, I should stop talking about Jenna. I'm not jealous of her or anything. I'm glad she's picked for some of the roles I go out for, because they are terrible 'B' rated movies. They make *Sharknado* look like a masterpiece. Yet she still gets work.

After about five minutes Jenna busts out the red door of the room, a disappointed look on her face, makes eye contact with me as she treads through the lobby and stomps out the door to the parking lot. I felt my jaw drop an inch, I had to tell myself to close my mouth. I would know that look anywhere. That was a bad audition look—a fucking what the fuck. I realized that this was my golden opportunity to make this performance perfect. All my training, all my personal experiences would lead to this moment. If they weren't interested in Jenna, then I had a shot at the role.

Diane shot out of the door and called my name, "Sara Mackenzie." I pulled my headphones out of my ears, rolled them up and put them in my purse. I walked through the door while eyes watched me from all around, probably thinking the same thing I thought about Jenna, except I'm not a bimbo looking to give blowjobs for a part. *No sarcasm here.* Sorry, was that too much? She did give one to get on an episode of Law and Order a couple years ago. Alright already, enough about Jenna, now is my time to put my work to the test.

ACT TWO

I PASSED FROM THE EVENLY lit, noisy lobby into a quiet, cold, dark room and stood on an 'X' marked on the floor in pink gaffer's tape. The silence was deafening as they say. It always was, never a peep until we started recording the audition.

The camera lens stared back at me like a mechanical eye that became a best friend I was never allowed to acknowledge. The black metal frame of the tripod held my friend to eye level. The microphone mounted on top of the camera pointed at me like a black, foamy, pool noodle. My nerves were heightened every time I walked into a room like this one. I was tickled with an unsettling jitter in my hands and feet that only were calmed through meditation. After a few years of going through this torture you think I would be used to it by now.

Soft light boxes lit my face evenly, and I began to sweat from the heat they projected on me. It was always odd to feel like the sun was shining directly on my face while indoors.

I stood on my mark on top of this dirty carpet that looked like the original one when this place was furnished back in the 1970's. I had no makeup on, and my hair pulled back into a ponytail. Toni, the character I am trying to portray is a bad ass that doesn't take shit from anybody. I really wanted this role because I felt like it was meant for me and only me. The fact that it was a Stanley Nigel film was a bonus.

Two dimly lit faces sat behind a monitor in the back corner of the room. Whispers carried faintly as I stood there in the awkward silence, the camera judged me with its giant eye open without a blink. My self-consciousness grew with every second waiting for the cue to begin. I wanted to put my choices to the test and show how I envisioned this character in this scene. This is what attracted me to acting to begin with–the ability to be anyone–different mind sets, and moods just based on experiences you have already had in life; the ability to turn the written word into a visual masterpiece with emotions. I could easily do injustice to a writer's intent of a character if I didn't make a strong enough choice. This was a great fear of mine while I dissected each screenplay that I read.

Diane slated me for the camera. She had me say my name, height, weight, the role I was auditioning for, and the agency I was a part of. This part was even weirder than acting because it was very formal and dry. *No improvising here, sorry.*

A voice called from the back telling us to begin. Could it be the director of the film? This was an indie film after all, most times the director would be in the room with the casting director to discuss the talent auditioned to call back later, if they were interested, if you were lucky enough.

Stanley Nigel wrote this screenplay called *Sea of Tranquility* about a woman who goes to jail for murdering the man that raped her. In the distant future this character is sent to the jail on the moon where convicts serve their life sentences.

I wanted this role so bad because I knew that this would become a cult classic if Stan made it like his last film, *The Watchers*. The film won some awards from a few film festivals, and that was his first feature film that was made for under one hundred thousand dollars. That is almost unheard of today. It was considered one of the most successful low budget films of all time. With the amount of people that worked on the film, and the action-packed scenes made, it looked like it was made for millions. This could make or break my career and I remembered back to the first audition: I had built up this image in my head of how my acting career was going to go. When I got in front of the camera, I immediately puked on the floor from my nerves getting to me. It took a long time for me to get back into acting after that.

"Alright, Sara, are you ready?" a man's voice called from behind the monitor.

"Yes," I responded, looking towards the dark corner where two heads glowed a shiny blue.

The digital chime of the camera and the red tally light came on to indicate I was now being recorded. I took a deep breath in and closed my eyes for a second to let the stress exit my body on exhaling before reopening my eyes to the bright lights on me. The last few years that I had been training, reading acting books about all the different styles of acting, all the plays I read, and the amount of crap I had auditioned for led to this moment.

In the jail cell on the moon, my character made a friend in the all women section of Tranquility prison. My character, Toni, sat on the bench in the prison yard when her friend, Brenda, came up to her midway through the script.

"Ready," Diane's voice calls to me in a calming, low tone. I nod my head.

"Toni, you got the plans yet?" Brenda takes a seat next to Toni. *Diane starts reading the script from behind the camera.*

"Yeah." Toni looks around the yard at the guards in the towers. *I scan the dark room like I'm looking for the guards. Squinting my eyes darting across the bright lights.*

"So how' we gettin' out of he-ah then?"

"What did I tell you before, Bren?" Toni (*Me*) says in a pissed off tone.

"Not to talk about dis shit in public," Bren repeats with a condescending tone.

"Come on, Bren." Toni slaps Bren in the chest, snapping Bren's attention, killing her negative attitude. *I lean over slightly and zip my lips tightly together and conjured a raspy whisper.* "You know that sick fuck, Warden Gregory is watching. He listens to everything out here, and you come up to me spitting shit?"

"I'm sorry, I'm just gettin' impatient." Bren rubs her chest gently and winces in pain.

"You wanna get us killed? That's what you're gonna do," Toni whispered to Bren.

"Hey, Toni, how did you like my fingers the other day?" Dido, a butch girl yells across the yard after a basketball rolls over to Toni's feet. Diane whisper-shouts from behind the camera. *In an earlier scene, Dido clocks Toni in the head in the shower after one of the guards left and molests her on the shower floor.*

I look off behind the camera and find a spot in the darkness where I could place Dido in the scene. My hands hit my chest and I flapped my arms outward, nodding my chin upward as I said my line:

"You can go fuck yourself, Dido!" Toni shouts back across the yard.

At this point in the scene, my character, Toni, and Dido get into a huge fight where I break her jaw on the bench and the guards bash me down with clubs until they knock me out.

"Thank you so much for coming in," the voice shouts out in the back of the room. I look towards the back and see the dim glow of the monitor. Diane stops the camera and the chiming sound dings again.

All that work to prepare for a short scene. I felt completely spent. I could swear I felt Toni living inside me at that moment. I wanted to punch someone in the head, and it felt like it should be Dido. I felt anger pent up inside me at that moment, like, this was it? This was the audition I gave to be shoved out of the room for the next woman to come in and possibly get the part over me?

At that moment I felt the emotional scars come back from the rape I survived when I was eighteen. I couldn't get the thought out of my mind. The feeling of helplessness from being drugged and taken advantage of. There was something wrong and I knew it, but I was incapacitated, watching my attacker as he thrust himself on top of me. I saw him talking, but words became just noise—gibberish I couldn't understand. All I remember was that I was at a party with my friend, Krista, and these guys were hitting on us. Then I remember feeling woozy and sitting down on a couch to relax for a minute. The next thing I knew I was in this room, it was dark, and I felt the flesh of someone else touching me. I opened my eyes and saw a blurry face and I tried to push him off, but I didn't have the strength. There was another man in the room, but he wasn't anywhere to be seen. I was reliving that moment, and I started to cry in front of everyone.

"Honey, don't worry, you did great," the voice projected from the back again. "We're going to call you, we promise." I couldn't help the way I felt right now. It was like I was a champagne bottle popped open and my emotions sprayed out, foaming onto the floor. My hands became the napkins for my tears.

"No, it's not that." My voice cracked and trembled. "Just some emotions that came from the character, that's all." I felt this urge inside me to storm out the door, there wasn't going to be a callback now. I was a hideous monster that just bawled my eyes out in front of these professionals. Maybe they have seen it before from people trying to get the gig, but that wasn't me, and I didn't want them to think that way about me. Diane came up to me and rubbed my back gently.

"It'll be alright, Sara," Diane said, handing me some tissues.

"Listen, why don't you take five minutes and come back and read from the scene on page thirty-seven," he spoke one last time. His voice became clearer, hearing it over again. I was able to pinpoint who was in the back of the room. Now I knew that this was Stanley Nigel, and he was talking to me. I looked at a reflection of light from his square framed glasses and nodded uncontrollably like a bobble head. I composed myself and gathered my things, and gradually walked out of the room.

"Thank you," I said as I exited into the lobby.

MORE GIRLS PILED IN through the door, giggling like this was a joke to even be here. With one fell swoop, I wanted to shut them up with a slap to the face. Life was a joke for some people, nothing was real to them, especially the ones that hadn't seen love die before their own eyes. There was a biker girl with tattoos, a nose ring, and a faded pink mohawk standing in the corner. She was probably going out for the role of Dido. I'm pretty sure it wasn't makeup and a wig she was wearing, and those tattoos looked real. I bet she's seen her share of death and destruction and she could probably kick my ass in a real fight if she wanted to.

I took a seat as Stephanie Garner was called into the room. Stephanie was the girl next door you wanted to be friends with because she had a lovely smile and a great sense of humor. She was about the same size as me too. Five foot-six and about a hundred and ten pounds, give or take a couple pounds. She seemed to be landing a lot of roles lately since she was on a few episodes of *Glow* on Netflix and *Supernatural* on the CW. Stephanie was making her way to becoming a good little character actor that was versatile and easy to cast because everyone loved her southern accent. She was from New Orleans and had done some good indie film work while she lived there. The door closed, I crossed my legs in my seat and looked over my lines in the script.

I focused on my work and grabbed at a few more character choices so that I could nail this next scene and get Stanley Nigel to cast me in this role. The giggles and chit-chat faded when I finely tuned my focus on my character's lines.

The soft glow of the fluorescent bulbs flickered on the white pages. I thought about this scene and it played over and over in my head. I kept thoughts in mind I would be able to access during the scene that would guarantee a realistic moment while on camera. The anger built up—the thought of the bastard who raped me flooded my mind. I couldn't use this choice for this character. Was it too soon? Would I ever get over this incident, or would it follow me around for the rest of my life? The feelings were so deep and organic I just let them flood over me. Hatred filled my heart and for a second, I forgot where I was and what I was doing. If I could take that man's life for what he did to me the same way that Toni does in this screenplay, maybe I would be happy. Maybe, I, too, would get over this feeling of emptiness inside me.

Why were men so cruel, I asked myself over, and over again. A question that most women probably have been asking themselves for centuries, but this is where it stops. If I could do something that would help young women today to avoid those situations I would totally act on that ambition. If it was single handedly murdering every rapist and child molester on this planet, then maybe that would be my superpower.

My heart was sinking in my chest when I thought about the aftermath of the raping. The trial that led to the accused man to get off free. Because I never really saw his face clearly, they couldn't prosecute him for the act without pure evidence that put him in the scene of the crime. I wanted to see him bleed, the red covered my hands as I held a knife, I embedded into his belly six, seven, eight times, repeatedly until he stopped breathing. I dreamt about killing him for years, taking his life for taking my son's. I'm still haunted and the only thing I can do is breathe through the pain.

ACT THREE

BEFORE I KNEW IT, I was called back into the room. Eyes stared me down, some perplexed on why I was going back in the room, and others knew that this was a good thing for me. When you're called back into the room, they know that you probably have the part. But that isn't always the case. It has happened to me before and they wound up going with Gwen Flanders who got the part in a horror film that wound up making over one hundred million worldwide.

I looked to the back where the director was, but this time he wasn't there. I didn't see the rims of his glasses reflecting the glow of the monitor. Where did he go? The lights blinded me from seeing in the darkness of the room. I saw an outline of a body behind the camera, a little different from Diane's. The maroon shoes slightly lit from overspill of light helped to identify a man's foot pointing at me. The red light turned on, and the camera chirped.

"Time to work your magic," Stanley called out from behind the camera. My ears perked up with the sound of his voice. A flood of emotions came to me, lots of good, euphoric language built in my psyche and I was able to evoke my choices like flowing water. I crumpled my lines in my hands and read from memory, I'd read this verse so many times that I was able to recite the piece as I saw it. I dug deep to an experience of mine that I chose to use during this scene, something with emotion and evocation.

I saw his tiny, little face. The way I held his head while he looked up at me, arms and legs stretching for the first time. His eyelids were like wrinkles of skin covering the windows to his world. His cries belted out and rang in my ears, the greatest sound I ever heard.

"What got you in here?" Stanley said softly, behind the camera.

"I did something I couldn't take back." *I bowed my head slightly. Brushed my dark brown curls behind my ear.*

"That's why we're all here, Toni," Stanley says as Bren from behind the camera.

"I didn't want it to be this way though." I found a spot in the corner of the room I focused on and my eyes watered up.

"He took everything from me. The things I loved most in my life. He took it all."

"That bastard got what was coming to him." I visualized the blanket wrapped around his tiny body like a butterfly in a chrysalis with a baby's face popping out the top. The sheer joy I felt holding him made me smile.

"There was a time when I would have said I had it all. The moon didn't seem so far away, and It felt like I could have touched it from where I was standing. But he took the thing that meant the most to me." *A tear shed from my eye.* Anger filled my heart when I thought about my little boy. What he could have been.

"The jury found him not guilty. He probably paid them all off. But I made sure justice paid him a visit." Eight years ago, I named my dead son Noah, and I couldn't say his name without bursting into tears.

"Well he deserved it then."

"I would serve my sentence 20 times over if it brought Chevy back, but it won't." My hands tensed up and I crumpled the paper in my hands, my jaw clenched, and I felt the memory of Noah push through my mind as he passed away in that incubator. A premature baby born with heart palpitations and underdeveloped lungs. He didn't have a chance of survival. I was only eighteen when I had him. My boyfriend Craig and I had a drunken mishap and I decided to go through with having the baby. I wanted to find the man that raped me that night, and I wanted to stick a knife into his abdomen and watch him die just like Toni did in this film. I wanted to be able to do that so badly. I wanted to jump out of my skin and find him spiritually and strangle the life out of him. Unfortunately, only in the movies do we get the satisfaction of revenge. My arms shook, and my teeth chattered. The lights felt like I was on the operation table in the hospital again.

"As long as I live, I will dedicate every waking breathe to Chevy, if it means I have to kill every mother fucker in this place."

"You have some foam around your mouth." Stanley said. It was the line, but I really was foaming from my mouth, too. I wiped the foam on my sleeve, anger built up inside of me.

"I'm getting out of this place. Are you going to help me?"

"Cut." Stanly clapped from behind the camera. "That was brilliant, Sara," he said, and stopped the camera. The red tally light disappeared as he stepped out onto the floor. His black framed glasses rested on his long nose and his beady eyes pinched together with a happy grin. All I could think about was my baby. I felt despicable for using the loss of my son for this role, but the pain it caused me deserved to be shown to relate to the pain that Toni felt for her son. I thought I would've given acting up forever because of what happened to me. It dragged me down and caused such pain for so long, but it was my mother and ex-boyfriend Craig that coerced me back into it because of my love for the craft.

I SWUNG THE DOOR OPEN to the blinding daylight outside the office building's sidewalk. Before I could get five steps out the door, I pulled my phone from my pocket and told Siri to call my mom. The phone rang a few times.

"How'd it go?" My mother answered the phone immediately as she always did after any audition of mine. I was filled with such excitement I felt like I was going to jump twenty feet into the air and continue bouncing along all the way to my car.

"I got the part! They stopped the auditions and went with me right there!" My excitement leapt through the phone.

"Oh my God, that is great!" Her voice scrambled with distortion over my receiver when she screamed into the microphone. I walked down the sidewalk to the parking lot filled with cars—the other girls leaving gave me dirty looks like I didn't deserve the part. *Fuck them* I thought, they had no idea what I went through to get this role.

"We will have to celebrate when we see you!" my mom said with a high-pitched tone of excitement.

"We will," I said

"When do you start shooting?"

"Next week in Atlanta."

"Amazing! We can meet you up there before you start shooting."

"Sounds good."

"I told you things would come together for you."

"Thanks, Mom. Make sure you tell Daddy, ok?"

"I will tell your father when he gets off work."

"Thanks, Ma." I opened the door to my ratty Toyota Tercel. Four different colors covered the hunk of rusted metal and faded plastic. The door always creaked and needed a good slam to stay shut. The window would fall when I did this. I wouldn't have to put up with this for much longer.

"Ok. Congrats, honey." I ended the phone call tossed my phone on the passenger seat. I cranked the manual window up and sat back in my seat reflecting on the rush I just had. I was excited, but I still wanted to cry, I couldn't stop thinking about Noah and how he wasn't here to celebrate this moment with me. He physically would never be here with me, but I liked to think that his spirit was with me whenever good things happened. My head leaned on the steering wheel as I wept into the warm plastic. A couple minutes went by and then I was touched by something that made me smile. The presence of love everlasting touched my shoulders and I felt like the clouds parted and shone some sunshine just on me at that moment. This was the beginning to something I had wanted for a long time. My love of cinema pushed me in this direction, and it was from here on out that my career of being an actor would be defined by being the lead female in a Stanley Nigel picture.

This time next year I could be on stage accepting an Academy Award for this performance. It was the thought of being without Noah, but the thought of him being with me forever in spirit that gave me the strength to continue forward.

The Path

INFECTIOUS LAUGHTER echoed deep in the forest along a leaf tattered path where a cottage rests on the outskirts of Cleveland in the North Georgia Mountains. Donna and Cheryl were two young girls full of imagination, chasing dreams of marrying their favorite princes inside magnificent castles. Donna's older sister, Cheryl, became like a mother—always giving direction and deciding what was right from wrong for Donna. Cheryl acted as commander-in-chief whenever their mother wasn't around which became apparent as each day passed. Even at a young age, Donna did as Cheryl asked. She trusted her big sister knowing that Cheryl would never steer her wrong.

The girls skipped along trails traveling deeper into the forest further away from their grandparent's cabin. Critters scurried at the sounds of their giddy laughs. Birds' wings fluttered—their nests left abandoned as they perched in high branches of the pines. Squirrels skittered up the bark watching with crooked necks as the girls hopped down the path. Donna and Cheryl came to a fork in the path that led through a large overgrown thorn bush.

"Donna, be careful," Cheryl demanded.

"I'm fine." Donna squeezed in between the opening of the thorn bushes to explore what was on the other side. "Are you coming?" Donna said after she crawled through, brushing the dirt off her knees.

"I'm right behind you." Cheryl squeezed through but caught her shirt on a thorn tearing a hole through the sleeve. "I told you I didn't want to go in here. Now my shirt is ruined." Cheryl wiped her hands on her shirt.

"I'll beat you to the end," Donna yelled back to Cheryl while running down the narrow path covered in weeds and low-lying branches.

"You know Grandpa told us not to go down here," Donna shouted at her sister.

"Stop being a ninny." Donna's voice carried in the distance followed by wild snickering.

The sun that lit the forest began to evanesce which left the path growing darker with every passing moment as day faded into night. Donna followed the path further down where she heard water trudging downstream. Cheryl caught up to Donna and stopped behind her. They walked out of the opening of the forest to a bed of stones on the outer banks of the creek, its snakelike pattern curved around large, jagged boulders protruding from the running water.

"A lady died here. Don't you remember the story?" Cheryl said.

"I think Grandpa made that up."

"Either way, he told us not to come down here."

"He probably thinks we will drown. I know how to swim." Donna inched her feet to the edge of the creek. The small stones under her feet made a grinding, clunky noise that she never heard before. She bent over and placed her hands in the cool water. The fresh mist filled her nostrils, she pleasantly wafted in the scent. Cheryl immediately grabbed Donna's shirt, so she wouldn't fall in.

"Let go of me!"

"No! I don't want you to fall in."

"I'm fine, Cheryl. I'm staying right here." Donna wanted to jump in the water so bad just to prove to her she could do it. She knew it wasn't that deep either, but that wasn't the point.

"I don't think it's a good idea."

"It's just a story, Cheryl." Donna pulled her shirt back.

"What if we see her?"

"The ghost?"

"I think we should get back. It's getting late and Grandma was making dinner for us. They will be wondering where we are." The tips of the pine trees became silhouettes in the afterglow of the sunset.

"Fine." Donna said, adjusting her shirt collar simultaneously.

Grandpa told Donna and Cheryl just a summer ago the dangers of the forest, and how there was sacred ground nearby where people were buried during the Civil War. There was one woman he talked about most of all. He had seen her ghost before walking through the forest and near the creek. Her name was May Stevens, the wife of George Stevens, a confederate soldier fighting in the war. When a courier brought the bad news that George been killed in battle, she fled her home where she left six children behind. She came down here to the creek where she leapt into the deepest part, sinking to the bottom, till her last bubble floated to the top and she drowned. Some say she couldn't take the burden of raising six kids by herself. Others said May knew that she had lost everything they had worked for and feared their house and their land would be taken from them. Others said she may have been possessed, driven to her death by the demon that lived inside her. No one knew the real story, but Grandpa said she took a life every year at the creek to share her sorrow of losing it all. The girls at this young age didn't fully understand the idea behind ghosts and what they truly meant, but they knew the story was meant to scare them into not going down by the creek.

Cheryl finally convinced Donna to leave the creek. While she dismounted the boulder and backed up from Donna, she saw something standing in the distance across the creek. A woman was standing on one of the boulders. There was something odd about her; she seemed very still and was creepily staring at them.

"Hello, miss." Cheryl said, waving her hand at her. Donna looked at the woman and noticed her moving closer to them, carefully walking across the boulders. The woman waved back.

"Can we help you, miss? You look lost." The woman's dress looked dated, like it was made in the 1800s.

"Will you girls follow me?" her soft raspy voice called out. She was getting closer and her features became clearly visible. Cheryl screamed when the woman's hair uncovered her face. A chill raised up Cheryl's spine, throwing her into panic mode—her legs turned before the rest of her body, running back towards the path.

Cheryl's scream startled Donna, watching her run off without her—Donna looked back over her shoulder and saw a deathly white woman soaking wet from head to toe gazing back at her. The woman extended her arm and held her hand out to Donna. She was almost close enough to touch her now.

"Come with me," the black haired, rotting flesh-faced woman said. Donna saw her eyes, how they were clouded over, her pupils barely visible. They looked like two eggs over easy, staring back at her. This must be May Stevens—the woman Grandpa was talking about. Donna froze and felt like she couldn't move, visually ingesting every detail of May Stevens' ghost. Her filthy, white dress billowed in the air like she was still floating in the water. It was unnatural for sopping wet fabric to float as it were dry. Donna also realized there wasn't any wind blowing.

Finally, Donna felt unfrozen and her vocal cords let out a scream that sent the nerves in her body a message to run. She followed Cheryl now darting back into the cover of the trees. Rocks shifted under her feet on her way up to the path. It felt like her feet were sinking into the ground, slowing her down. Her heart accelerated faster than she ever felt before. Tiny hairs on her arms raised and her skin was covered in goosebumps. Donna couldn't help but to turn her head before she entered the forest, May's eyes stretched open as far as they could go, reaching her stiff arm—fingertips shaking—then she vanished like the mist of water rising into the air.

Cheryl stopped at the thorn bush leading back to their grandparent's cottage. She bent her back forward held her hands on her knees, taking deep breathes. Donna stomped up the dirt path and stood beside Cheryl throwing her arm over her slumped back sucking in all the air she could.

"Did–you–see–that?" Donna said a word in-between each breath.

"That's why I ran." In the distance Cheryl heard a faint bell ringing. It was almost dark. Their grandmother had probably been ringing the bell for the past fifteen minutes.

"Don't tell Gram and Pa-Pa about going to the creek. They will never let us out of the cottage again," Donna begged Cheryl.

"Fine, but we never go down there again. Promise?" Cheryl stood erect, Donna's arm falling back to her side.

"Promise." Cheryl linked pinkies with Donna. Cheryl proceeded to squeeze through the bush followed by Donna. They didn't make it too far down the path when their grandfather ran into them just over a hill about fifty yards from the thorn bush.

"You girls have nearly scared your grandmother and I half to death. Where have you two been?" He looked down at them with a mix of fright and anger written all over his face.

"Sorry Pa-Pa. We got lost, exploring a little further off the path than normal," Cheryl said.

"You didn't go to the creek, did you?" He looked at them with a half-squinted eye.

"No. We were having too much fun pretending we were princesses. We didn't hear the bell," Donna said looking up to her grandfather's darkened face. Most of his salty hair was covered by his favorite herringbone flat cabbie.

"Let's go home. It's dark out here and I'm sure my princesses are hungry." He threw his arms around their shoulders and walked with both girls on either side of him.

"Do you think Prince Henry will take me to the ball, Cheryl?" Donna popped her head past her grandfather's pot-belly and looked over to Cheryl.

"He would be mad not to." Cheryl skipped ahead. Donna followed her lead. Grandpa looked at the two and smiled, placing his hands in his pockets.

"I want to get married one day and live in a castle just like Cinderella."

"Can I live with you?"

"I guess so. But you will have to live in the guest house." They all laughed. The girls ran ahead of grandpa and up the stoop of the cottage—the door flung open chaotically with a slam.

Every time Donna closed her eyes, she was haunted by May Stevens' face. It spooked her when she thought about it.

"Where were you two? Are you alright Donna? Looks like you just saw a ghost." Donna looked at Cheryl but didn't say a word. Grandma waited a second for a reply, but both the girls hushed up like they never heard what grandma said to begin with.

"Supper is getting cold," Grandma said, placing the two big cups of milk in her hands on the table. Donna and Cheryl chugged the milk like they hadn't had a drink in a week. The cups tipped upside down over their faces and they slammed them to the table almost simultaneously, white liquid mustaches coated above their lips.

"Sit down and eat you two." Grandma's voice echoed out the door.

Grandpa paused at the stoop. He felt a presence, like someone was watching him. He cocked his head behind him, watching the path for some movement, but he only saw the leaves on the branches, rustling in the wind. The sun had sunk below the horizon and the path became a blackened wall of trees. He turned to the cottage and walked inside where the girls were shoveling their meal into their mouths as quickly as they could. Grandpa laughed and shut the door.

AFTER A COUPLE OF DAYS in the first week of summer, Donna and Cheryl knew how to navigate through the foliage covered hills that surrounded them. Only being three years apart, Cheryl was Donna's best friend. Living in Atlanta, Donna was mostly on her own. Each morning Cheryl helped by making two bowls of cereal for breakfast and reminding Donna to brush her teeth before they left for school. Mom and Dad woke the girls up before leaving for work, so they could get to school on time.

Mom was a waitress at the local airport diner where she opened at five in the morning. Dad was the first man in his family to go to college and became a high school English teacher. Donna spent lots of time with her sister at the high school after elementary let out. They walked from their school to spend the afternoon in the empty halls. Donna loved to jump rope in the gymnasium, so Cheryl would take her where they spent the afternoon jumping rope together. Sometimes Dad dropped them off at the diner to spend time with Mom when he coached during basketball season. Every night after they finished their homework, Donna and Cheryl helped clean dishes and brought pie to customers for dessert. The tips for mom were always big whenever the girls were around.

Donna and Cheryl saw their grandparents some weekends, the holidays, but always looked forward to spending the sum-

mer with them. One of Donna's most distinguishable memories was the smell of breakfast cooking in the morning.

Donna sprinted out of bed, her little feet pattering across
the floor to Cheryl's bed, excitedly jolting her awake. Donna
ran as fast as her legs could carry her downstairs to the kitchen.
Giggling all the way down, racing Cheryl to the table to de-
termine the winner. Grandma smiled like a crescent moon, her
eyes became little buttons surrounded by doughy rose-colored
flesh, cued by earthquakes buzzing through the ceilings, shaking glasses in cabinets, and rattling porcelain collectable figures
along the fireplace mantle. Hot breakfast would be served by
the time they made it to the chairs. Bacon, eggs, toast, and a
glass of orange juice were inhaled in seconds.

One summer Donna had an idea to mark the trees, so they
wouldn't get lost again. They found the sharpened knife in
grandpa's office desk drawer, a gift given to him by his boy scout
troop when he retired 10 years earlier as troop leader. Donna
remembered holding the wooden handle with *Troop 112* en-
graved into the wood. Grandpa left most of his knives locked
up in a cabinet, but not his trusty pocketknife. Donna and
Cheryl took turns the whole day marking the trees that led
home. This helped them get home quicker in the late evening
for supper—before the sky would fade to darkness. Grandma
rang the bell to come home for dinner and they would race
back to the cottage, following the *X's* they had made in the bark
of the trees.

Even though they had been told never to go down to the
creek, Donna wanted to go back to see May Stevens' ghost
again. She always seemed to creep up on them at twilight. Donna felt the presence of May's ghost floating around the for-

est—heard her voice calling to her in the wind, but never saw her since the day at the creek. When Grandpa found the girls markings the trees with his knife, his happy-go-lucky attitude turned into a stern tone.

"I'm disappointed in you little ladies." He bent down with a moan, his industrial grade Maglite held in his hand slumped over one knee, looking Donna in her eyes.

"You girls shouldn't use knives at your age. You could've hurt yourselves." His pointer finger extended in their direction. "You also hurt those trees by doing that."

"The trees can't feel, Grandpa," Cheryl said.

"All living things feel, Cheryl." The girls looked at each other. Their faces were perplexed with the idea that the trees were alive. Donna was touched with a guilt, but the damage had already been done. Grandpa felt he made his point. He hugged them, one in each arm, pulled them close and let go.

Although Donna grew up in the city with her family, she grew fond of her grandparent's cottage and when she was a teenager, her and Cheryl spent less time at the cottage. She wanted to spend more time with her grandparent's but life with friends, school, and working as a barista at a local coffee shop kept her planted in the city. Shortly after Donna's twenty-first birthday, Grandpa passed away followed by Grandma only six months later from a broken heart. The cottage was left to Donna and Cheryl in their grandparents' will.

A few months after grandma's passing, with the help of Mom and Dad, the family cleaned up the cottage, working on the weekends to get rid of the things they wouldn't keep in the home. Donna and Cheryl reminisced about the fun times they had during the summer when they were kids.

Donna and Cheryl opened a coffee shop together off the interstate on the way up to the cottage and called it D&C's Coffee Haven. After a few years the business was doing well, and they had been living in the place that they grew up loving. Donna still had this feeling while being at the cottage, especially early in the morning someone or something was watching her. She heard voices echo through the forest, soft ethereal voices that sounded as if they were saying *follow me*. Donna remembered May's ghost saying that to her on that day at the creek. Since then, she avoided the creek, even with superstitions and logical explanations, she coerced herself into believing she made it up. Donna got spooked by the thought of May's ghost.

A MISTY FOG GENTLY hovered through the forest like a low-lying cloud. The path was a maze that sunk and rose through the hilly terrain. Donna's breath looked like steam from a kettle in the cool autumn air. It was six weeks till winter, and the frigid weather was tiptoeing its way south. Her morning run became a routine to clear her mind, so she could retain focus for the day ahead. Trees contorted their long limbs—reaching down like hands yearning to touch her.

Donna thought she caught a glimpse of a white, silky dress vanishing behind a tree once before. This time she saw a profile of a woman crossing the path in the distance. She blinked her eyes rapidly and thought the fog had her seeing things. She stopped ahead and there wasn't any indication that the path had been crossed. Her heart rate rose, blood pumped at an accelerated rate. Some of the strands of her hair had fallen out of her ponytail, and she pulled the elastic band out of her hair, continuing to pull her hair back neatly, securing the loose strands. Rapid breaths filled her lungs as she turned to the path that led down to the creek. She thought of that time her and Cheryl ventured down this path all those years ago and what she saw. The rustling of water beating the hard surfaces of boulders could be heard in the distance. The creek got louder with every step she took, her shoes sank into the mud, and her clothes became scratched and torn by the sharp, overgrown limbs that clawed at her like cats on a scratching post. When Donna stepped out of the finite path, she smelled the fresh water as the mist licked her face. The sun made its way above the horizon, pulverizing the fog. The glistening reflection of the sunrise forced her to squint her eyes. With her hand extended, she shaded the sun to see the slithering creek bend and curve its way south. She squinted and saw a dark silhouette of somebody standing in the distance. The hazy glow of the sun made it hard to see clearly.

"Hello!" she said, blocking the sun with her hand as much as she could. There wasn't a reply. "What are you doing out here?" She took short steps to get a better view. Still nothing. A couple steps closer she found the shade of a tree where her vision was cleared. Looking at the top of the bolder she saw May in her white gown looking at her as a lively young woman. Something was wrong though, her face was distraught, she looked sad and wept. May stepped off the rock and splashed into the water. Donna's face lost its rosy hue, turning white. She immediately ran to help. Donna came upon the rocks that cut through the creek and followed it to where May leapt off. Nothing there. The woman was nowhere to be found. Not a sound, not even a yelp. Donna kneeled over and looked in the shallow water. Where she could have gone? She just vanished. Terror crawled over Donna's face as she searched downstream looking for a sign of life. She got off her hands and knees and backed away from the creek. Looking around frantically to see if she could see kicking around somewhere in the water. There wasn't a trace of anyone. Donna wondered if she had been seeing things again. Was it May's ghost showing her how she died? After a few moments of gathering her thoughts, she picked herself up and took in deep breaths again as she remembered how to breath.

Her flushed face regained its rosy glow as she glanced at her watch. It was a quarter after seven and the timer continued to advance on her Apple watch. Donna spun around and ran back up the path she followed down to the creek. When she reached the path that led back to the cottage, she noticed the scarred *X* on the tree she leapt out from behind. She fingered the smooth surface surrounded by rough bark. She didn't remember marking this tree as a child.

Donna continued at a steady pace—she tried to forget what she might have seen, pushing the panicked thoughts out of her mind. She couldn't help but to think of May Stevens, and how she died in the creek.

Gusts of wind blew across the path, and in Donna's ears, a voice whistled in the breeze—sounding like soft ethereal echoes whispering her name. Donna's heart pounded harder, she felt it clawing at her chest—increasing speed. *Follow me, the voice called out.*

Cutting through the path at twice the speed as normal, she reached the edge of the cottage property at an incredible pace.

She keeled over in front of the stoop, using the banister for support, she gasped—filling her lungs with much needed oxygen. Wiping sweat from her forehead with the ends of her shirt, she climbed the steps to the front door and walked in.

Cheryl came down the stairs in her pajamas, her hair a mess and crust still in her eyes.

"Good morning. I was just heading up to surprise you," Donna said, hiding the fright that plagued her mind.

"I don't know how you do it every morning."

"It's refreshing, better than a cup of coffee?" Donna said nonchalantly.

"Speaking of which, can you put a pot on for me?"

"I already did."

"Such a good sister." Cheryl patted Donna on the shoulder as she walked past her to the coffee pot, opened the cabinet, and pulled out a mug.

"I know. You don't have to tell me twice."

"Knew it'd go to your head, forget I said anything."

"You should go for a run with me in the mornings. It would be good for you."

"No way. Don't pull me into that shit. You like running. I like coffee." Cheryl poured the hot black liquid into a coffee mug that said *'When life hands you coffee beans... Make Coffee! - D&C's Coffee Haven'.*

"Fine. A girls gotta try."

"Try all you want but this girl's set in her ways." Cheryl took a sip from the mug after blowing on it multiple times.

"Hey, I got to tell you something." Donna turned to Cheryl with a nervous grin on her face.

"What?"

"Remember when we were kids and we went down to the creek?"

"Uh...Yeah. How could I ever forget that day?" Cheryl walked to the fridge, opened it up, and grabbed the creamer.

"Right, well..." Donna thought about how she was going to tell Cheryl that she was just down at the creek by herself and saw May jumping into the water, but she stopped herself.

"Well, what?" Cheryl poured the creamer into the mug in front of the kitchen window. After she was done, she looked out and saw a woman in the distance looking at her.

"What the fuck?" Cheryl said, squinting her eyes.

"What happened?" Donna said. Cheryl turned to look at Donna, and when she looked back, the woman was gone. Cheryl frantically looked around out all corners of the window and ran to the front door, still in her pajamas, no socks or shoes. She opened the door and walked onto the patio.

"What's going on Cheryl?" Donna followed her out the front door. Cheryl was quiet and didn't say a word. She stared off in the distance, scanning the trees, and eyeing the path leading into forest.

"Are you ok, Cheryl?" Donna touched her shoulder.

"Yeah. You didn't happen to see anyone, did you?"

"Well that's sorta what I wanted to talk to you about."

"What do you mean?" Cheryl said, facing the forest.

"Maybe we should go inside and sit down first."

"Yeah. Yeah. Good idea." Cheryl seemed to be preoccupied, almost dismissive to the request to come inside. Donna turned and walked in the door.

"As I was saying earlier about us as kids by the creek... I went down there this morning for some reason. I felt like something led me there and then I saw her." Donna walked back into the kitchen talking to Cheryl, thinking she was behind her, but she didn't come back in the house. When there wasn't an answer, Donna turned back around and saw she was alone in the house. She was confused and annoyed she was talking to herself. She walked back out the door and saw Cheryl walking down the path, in her pink pajamas, barefoot.

"Where are you going Cheryl?" Donna called out. Cheryl continued forward like she didn't hear her. Donna crept down the steps of the cottage and followed Cheryl down the path. Leisurely Cheryl meandered down the path, her bare feet sinking into the muddy sediment. The trees engulfed her as she descended deeper into the forest. Donna kept her distance, watching in wonderment of Cheryl's hypnotic state. Donna called out to her again but still no answer. Donna's feet quickened to catch up to Cheryl. She was right behind Cheryl as she stopped in front of the overgrown thorn bush, studying the crowded passageway where the path led to the creek.

"Cheryl? What are you doing?" Donna placed her hand on Cheryl's arm, her body was still and cold, her feet planted as roots in the soil. She swayed intensely in an unpleasant. Donna walked in front of her and caught a glimpse of a wide-eyed stare perpetually unfocused. She snapped her fingers three times in Cheryl's face, not even a blink. Her neck stretched forward, her face pushing closer to Cheryl's while grabbing at her arms making her body quake.

Cheryl thrust her hands to Donna's throat in an instant, applying enough pressure to cut off her air supply. Donna's face transformed from bright red to a ripe plum. Her eyes bulged—blood vessels swollen—pupils fluttered backward toward her skull. Cheryl's face was flat as a calm sea, emotionless and unchallenged as she gripped tighter with the strength of two people. Failing to break Cheryl's grip, Donna could feel she was about to pass out so, she released her hands from Cheryl's grip with a swift punch to her breast. Cheryl's grip loosened, and her hand flew to her injured breast. Donna gasped for air intensely. The purpled color flushed back to a healthy shade of pink in moments of oxygen re-entering the blood stream. Cheryl winced in pain and moaned out loud.

"What the hell did you hit me for?" Cheryl cried out, turning around, tucking her hands under her armpit and under her breast.

"You were choking me." Donna said, regaining her breath.

"Are you out of your mind?" Cheryl spun around completely perplexed. "Why are we in the forest?" She glanced down at her feet covered in mud. "Where are my shoes?"

"I followed you here. You said you saw something. I turned around and you were halfway down the path and you stopped here." Donna put her hands on her knees and bent over gulping air.

Cheryl couldn't remember anything. She looked back down the path toward the cottage, she looked back at Donna terrified, eyes wide open in disbelief.

"I started to choke you?"

"Yeah. What were you doing?"

"One minute I was in the kitchen talking to you, next minute I'm out here with my breast in severe pain." Caressing her breast over her shirt, her face scrunched to one side.

"I'm sorry but you were literally going to kill me if I didn't do something."

"Maybe a kick to the shin would have been fine."

"Next time you're being choked out, let me know what you think of first." Donna's sarcasm inched between her shallow breaths.

"Sorry." Cheryl made that face whenever she apologized. She furrowed her brows, forehead wrinkled up, and her lips protruding from her face.

"It's fine." Cheryl took her hands off her breast and stepped closer to Donna who slid her hands off her knees exhaling a giant breath. Her hands massaged her throat unintentionally as she erected her spine.

"I saw her." Cheryl looked away from Donna.

"May Stevens?"

"She was outside the window. That's the last thing I remember."

"I saw her earlier, when I went down to the creek."

"I thought you weren't going to go down there again!"

"I just had to see if..."

"If what? The crazy ghost lady would kill you. Or me?" Cheryl shouted at Donna.

"That was so long ago, I didn't know if it was real." Donna tried to convince herself she was being sane by looking for trouble.

"It was real, Donna. At least it felt that way to us as kids."

"I know but..."

"I still have nightmares of that woman's face. I wake up in the middle of the night and I can't go back to sleep. Sometimes I don't even know why I moved out here because it haunts me so much."

"We will be fine, Cheryl."

"How do you know, Donna?" Donna struggled for an answer. "I loved being here during the summers. I completely forgot about it for a long time, probably because we were busy with our lives, but I feel her calling me more and more recently. I don't know how much longer I can resist."

Donna shook her head at Cheryl, biting her lip as she fought away some tears. Donna didn't want Cheryl to feel this way, and she didn't want her led to death by a ghost either.

"Are we crazy?" Donna said.

"What do you mean?"

"Listen to us. We're talking about a ghost. Like there's nothing we can do."

"I don't know. It just seems so real."

"I used to think Grandpa was telling us that story for us to stay away from the creek, so we wouldn't get hurt or drown, but now I really think he knew something that we didn't."

"Maybe he did. I used to watch him looking over his shoulder while we played together. He stared at someone for long periods of time but there was no one ever there."

Donna remembered her grandfather acting strange sometimes while they played in the forest. She remembered when he found them in the forest that night they got lost, worried half to death, his face paler than a can of white paint. May Stevens' ghost haunted the creek and the surrounding areas for over one hundred and fifty years, but Donna knew that her and Cheryl would be safe. If her grandpa and grandma lived here all these years and nothing happened to them, they should be fine.

"Let's get back. We have to get to work." Donna smiled and slung her arm over Cheryl's shoulder. The two sisters walked down the path to the cottage holding each other close. Donna knew the only way to defeat May was to completely forget about her. Keep her furthest from their memories and they would be alright. As the sisters traveled closer to their cottage, May's ghost moved through the thorn bush and followed them down the path.

Venus and the Galaxy

STRANGERS ALWAYS ATTRACT to each other in different ways. I believe that we all have this magnetism that draws us together in a time and place that most would call fate. Fate is a funny word because it exemplifies that events in a person's life are out of their hands. We cannot control the aspects of our life that may be left up to a supernatural being, or the positive or negative energies of the universe. I am just a boy, lost in the world—soaring through an ever-expanding galaxy among galaxies. I felt insignificant, I felt lost, I felt rejected most of my life. I felt that I would never make a difference to anyone. I was lost. I didn't know I could be found, until I met her.

High school always seemed to be a bore, just a place I would have a snooze fest. The only thing that made me keep going is knowing I was going to see Venus in astronomy class. I don't want to brag or anything, but I am a little smarter than the average student body, which meant most the times the jocks and the bullies would pick on me and the other nerds like me. Maybe one day I would go into outer space, visit the moon or mars and show everyone that they were messing with an interstellar voyager. I doubt they would say anything more than, oh hey, there's that kid from high school we used to stuff in the lockers during gym.

Venus was one of these people too, but she was more than just a nerd, she was smart, beautiful, and had a ton of friends. How could she be so great and not even know I existed? Or at least I thought she didn't. I sat towards the back of the classroom where models of the solar system hung from the ceiling and posters of planets and galaxies were thumbtacked to the corkboard like walls. One day Mr. Fletcher called on me to answer the average distance between the sun and the earth. *Approximately 93 million miles.* Venus looked back at me with a semi-funny grin, almost creepily staring at me, but she turned back to face Mr. Fletcher. That was the best day of my life so far and I couldn't tell you what that meant but I think I was floating when I saw Venus look at me the way she did. I hated being called on in the middle of class, but I was glad that Mr. Fletcher was trying to catch me daydreaming that day.

My friend, Pauly, knew how I felt for Venus, and every day in the lunchroom he would have to snap his fingers in front of my face to get my attention as she walked across the room to her friends and her boyfriend at the cool kids table. Her boyfriend looked like a young Pharrell Williams, and he knew this, so he wore weird hipster hats to play the part. Ronny was his name and he was talented, he could spit rhymes like his predecessor, make music, and play sports. So, all wins for Ronny, and the winning smile he wore made it easy for a girl like Venus to fall in love with him.

Things changed one day after school for me while I was working at the local Green Market that was about a mile walk from school and only three blocks away from my home. I stocked the shelves daily, hauled pallets of food through the loading bay, and unloaded the boxes carrying meats, cheeses, milk, vegetables, juices, frozen goods, pretty much anything you could think of. Each morning we received a delivery of these items where the produce clerk Wesley would stock some of the shelves during the day, and I finished unpacking the contents after I clocked in for the night shift. I would stack the food items on a steel U-Boat utility cart and make my way out to the coolers and aisles to stock the shelves. The cart I used always had an annoying wheel that rattled, making it noticeable that I was in the market. I set up in front of the aisles that needed restocking, cut open the boxes, and placed the items on the shelves. Cans of vegetables, beans, boxes of pasta, crackers, cereal, coffee, bags of potato chips—the list goes on.

The aisles had been freshly waxed the night before by the night crew and the shine of the terrazzo flooring glistened with the reflection of the fluorescent warehouse lights hung from the rafters of the ceiling. I had opened a box with my blade and was pulling bottles of strawberry Powerade out and placing them on the shelf when I saw Venus. It was like time had stopped, the electrons in the air sparked and bolted in random jolts— my focus yanked by the curves of her body to a gorgeously sculpted face. Her sneakers squeaked on the waxed floor—my heart rate spiked, my nerves twitched as she walked towards me like everything was recorded in 240 frames per second and played back in slow motion. She wore an oversized, denim, button-down shirt that was covered by a black leather jacket and tight black pants. The lopsided, black beanie rested on top of her strawberry colored hair with light blonde tips. She had these mirrored aviator sunglasses on which let me believe she didn't give a damn what people thought of her. I felt my mouth droop uncontrollably, my blood thickened so heavily it was if I could feel it course through my veins, causing me to sweat while thinking of what to say to her. She stopped and stood next to me.

"Wait, don't I know you?" Venus said, pulling her sunglasses off her face and resting them on her beanie. Her green eyes stabbed at me. My mouth went dry and I felt like I was going to pee my pants at any moment now.

"Um... Yeah..." I cleared my dry throat. Closing my eyes, I tried to vision I was talking to someone else, maybe Pauly, or my mom. Eww, not my mom, that made this even weirder.

"Yeah, uh... we have astronomy together." I winced and opened my eyes to see her still standing there. I wasn't dreaming at all. This was totally real.

"Oh. Yeah. You're the 93 million miles guy."

"Yes!" I blurted out with excitement, surprised that she remembered me. Venus backed up a step, looking frightened. "Yes," I whispered, "that was me." And then, I continued to laugh nervously.

"You are a weird kid, you know that?" She cocked her head and squinted like she was trying to see through to my soul. "I didn't know you worked here," she said, folding her arms together.

"Up until now I didn't know you knew I existed." The words spilled out of my mouth like I was having a brain malfunction. "Sorry."

"Woah. You must think pretty low of me."

"No-no-no-no-no, that's not it at all," I rushed out as quickly as I could say the words.

"So, what then? You have a secret hate society for me or something?"

"Oh my god, quite the opposite," I said, not thinking about anything I was saying.

"Wait, what?" She looked so confused right now. I could imagine what my face looked like from her view, a dude with googling eyes not blinking, and my mouth drooping to the floor like I had tried to lift weights with my teeth. I had no idea what to say right now, I was completely dumbfounded. I had a crush on this girl for months and I completely sold myself out in less than thirty seconds of talking to her. What the heck was I thinking?

Just as I was about to profess my love for her and how I couldn't get her out of my mind—Pharrell, I mean Ronny came around the corner of the aisle calling out to Venus.

"There you are, I was looking all over the store for you." Ronny walked up to her and put her arm around her. "What are you doing?" he said looking at her then at my stunned face. "Is he ok?"

"Yeah, I was just asking where the strawberry Powerade was."

"It's right there." Ronny looked at the shelf and pointed at it. "He's got boxes of it right there on the cart too." She looked puzzled and I wasn't going to say anything now that Ronny was standing in front of the two of us.

"Thanks, babe," she said and smiled at him.

"Do you know this guy?" he said with the most awkward look I've ever seen someone give before. For some strange reason I thought this was the time to extend my hand and introduce myself like he was the father of my bride to be.

"Cillian. Nice to meet you, sir." He shook my hand unwillingly with a confused look on his face. "We have astronomy class together. Nothing more than that really. Just noticed each other, that's all that is going on here." I finished shaking Ronny's hand and looked at Venus and winked.

"Why did he just wink at you?"

"I don't know. He's just a little weird that's all. This is the kid I was telling you about."

"Oh, the smart kid that gets all the answers right in class." Ronny's face lit up with realization.

"Yeah, that's him." Venus plainly stared at me.

"Well that explains it." Ronny looked me up and down quickly like I was some sort of freak. They were also talking about me like I wasn't standing there at that moment, but I continued to listen and kept my mouth shut.

"Do you think you're going to go to outer space one of these days? Work for NASA or something like that?" Venus said to me. She asked the first real question I could answer without putting my foot in my mouth.

"Uh, well... That's the plan I guess." And that was the only thing I could think of.

"Looks like he belongs in outer space." Ronny turned to Venus, whispering in her ear but I heard what he said.

Venus turned to him and slapped his arm as he laughed with his dumb Pharrell look-a-like hat on. I wanted to knock it off his tiny head.

"That wasn't nice."

"Can we go now, or did you have a homework question to ask Mr. space balls over here?" Ronny pointed at me and giggled.

"No," Venus replied to Ronny. She looked at me. "I'll see you in class tomorrow, right?" she asked as if she was anticipating on talking to me tomorrow.

"Yeah. I'll be there." I smiled but I'm sure it looked like I was dangling my teeth from my mouth in her direction.

Ronny turned around and started walking towards the registers. Venus grabbed the strawberry Powerade off the shelf and mouthed the word "sorry" while walking backwards and in one smooth swoop, she turned around and walked down the aisle.

My heart was beating so fast I felt the veins in my head pulsate. I felt light-headed, and dizzy, and I passed out in the aisle. I awoke in the arms of Charlie the Bakery Manager who always looked a little like the Pillsbury doughboy to me. I also think he might be a child molester because he always seemed to have a thing for me.

"You ok, little buddy?" Charlie said, cradling me in his arms.

"Yeah, I'm fine." I pushed myself out of his arms. I was surrounded by a few grocery clerks, cashiers, and one or two customers that just wanted to see what was going on. There were tiny whispers spreading amongst them.

I got up and walked out of the aisle to be alone for a moment with my thoughts. I couldn't believe that just happened with Venus. What was I going to tell her tomorrow when I saw her? I was so nervous that I was going to blow up my cover, but what was I hiding from anyways? Maybe this was my chance to really tell her how I felt. Maybe she would ditch the really handsome, super talented, Pharrell look-a-like just for me. I've been dreaming all this time, maybe it was about time I made my dreams come true, right?

THE NEXT DAY WHEN THE bell rang, I walked the crowded high school halls, dreading the conversation I would have with Venus. I'd been walking around like a zombie all day, mindlessly thinking about what I was going to say to her—trying to come up with some sort of excuse for the words that fell out of my mouth last night. *Maybe she forgot about what I said already,* I told myself.

Math class was a blur and I could only recall fragmented pieces of U.S. history class where Mrs. Goldstein wrote every stupid word I said last night on the board. *She definitely didn't forget.* The curly haired sixty-five-year-old that didn't want to retire from teaching because she loved it so much— shapeshifted into Venus—stood in front of the class and asked me what was the opposite of a hate club? I was mortified while I sat in that uncomfortable fold over desk chair that had been sitting in that same room since 1980. I was sweating so profusely, Jen Daniels, sat across from me, asked if I was going to barf.

I finally made it to the classroom and sat in my seat, Venus hadn't shown up yet. I was hoping maybe, just maybe, she took off today to go to the beach or something. As I was thinking that, she walked into the classroom and sat in the seat in front of me where Mike Delong usually sits. She turned her head towards me, my eyes diverted to the carving in my desk that said *FUCK U!* probably written by an angsty eighteen-year-old jock from 1980 as well.

"Hey," Venus said to me. I could see her body skewed toward me in my peripherals. I tried to ignore her like I was invisible. *Maybe she didn't see me.*

"Cillian," she said firmly. Her hand slapped on my desk where I was looking. I looked up to the most beautiful pair of eyes, green swallowing a yellow ring circling around her irises

"Oh, hey. How are you?" I played coy now. I wanted to put off the inevitable conversation for as long as possible.

"Good. Good. So about yesterday?"

"What about it?"

"Are you going to pretend you didn't say what you said to me?"

"Are we going to ask a bunch of questions right now that no one is going to actually have an answer for?" I said sarcastically, with a nervous chuckle, hopefully buying me some time before class started. Mike walked in the classroom and looked at Venus in his seat talking to me. He had this look on his face that said what the fuck is going on right now? If he came out and said it, that is. His upper lip looked like a hook snagged it and he squinted his eyes with a cold stare. I think he may have been a little jealous—at the same time scared for me because he knew what I was capable of. Mike walked over slowly behind Venus. Hoping this was my saving grace, my eyes widened as he approached. He held his books at his side and his bookbag strung over his shoulder.

"What is going on with your eyes?" Venus said.

"What? Oh nothing. Just a condition I have."

"Whatever. Please tell me what you meant yesterday about me not knowing you exist and that you feel the opposite of a hate club." She looked at me with these generic puppy dog eyes, something she probably did very often to get what she wanted from just about everyone that meant anything to her to get her way. It was working on me because I was about to spill the beans. Excuse the cliché, but that is what I was about to do. Mike finally walked up to the chair and she looked up at him.

"Can I help you?" she said like he was going to ask her to the prom or something.

"You're sitting in my seat." He pointed to the seat and looked at me.

"Oh, yeah. Sorry. Just one minute," she said to Mike and looked back at me. "So?" Mike huffed and stood there awkwardly. He didn't know what to do while Venus waited for me to tell her my biggest secret that really wasn't much of a secret to anyone but her, I guess. All my friends knew I had a crush on her. Even Mike stood there with his eyebrows raised, waiting for me to say something to her.

"I...Um...I really li..." Just then Mr. Fletcher came in and I was saved.

"Alright, folks. Get to your seats." He looked back at Mike hovering over Venus and me.

"Mr. Delong, please find a seat."

"But she's in my seat, sir."

"There is another seat up front here, Mr. Delong. You don't have a monopoly over that seat do you?"

"Uh...No."

"Then take the seat." Mr. Fletcher pointed to the seat and Mike reluctantly walked over to the seat while Venus turned her head back to me.

"This isn't over Cillian." She said waving with her index finger like she was reprimanding me like a mother.

I threw my head and body to the back of the chair a little frightened because I knew she knew this was just intermission to this horror show. *Why was I making a big charade out of this?*

Why couldn't I be honest with her? I sat at my desk nervous as shit, not paying attention to anything but the passengers on my shoulders telling me two different things, playing out two different scenarios of what could happen. Mr. Fletcher was doing some sort of lesson plan, but all I remembered him saying was something about Ursa Major. Venus turned around slightly and gave me a handwritten note. That's when Mr. Fletcher called on me.

"What do you think, Cillian?" Mr. Fletcher said, looking at me as if he'd caught me red-handed stealing the candy out of the jar.

"About what?" I said, stuttering, buying myself some time.

"What is Ursa Major?" I knew I heard him say that.

"It is known as the great bear, also known as the largest constellation of eighty-eight modern constellations and among the original forty-eight listed by Ptolemy in the AD second century. It is mainly comprised of the asterism of the seven bright stars of the big dipper."

"Ok," Mr. Fletcher said, disappointed for the missed opportunity to catch someone not paying attention in class. At that moment the class applauded, I stood up, took a bow, and Venus grabbed the back of my head, pulled my lips to hers, and passionately made out with me. Or I wish that's how it went. Mr. Fletcher went back to the lesson plan and I looked down at the letter on my desk and unfolded it. Her handwriting was rounded and colored in purple ink. It was so fancy, I wished my handwriting was this legible. Mine was like chicken scratch that no one, not even myself could read.

I thought since I can't seem to get you to talk to me physically, maybe I can get something out of you in a written note. I don't know why it bothers me, what you said yesterday. I don't think of myself as a girl that doesn't notice people, but it is hard to not notice you.

I couldn't believe what I was reading right now. Was the world turning upside down on its head where I was the king for a day or was I going mad? I continued to read the note.

You seem like such a smart guy, I'm afraid I'm going to humiliate myself in front of you.

I believe that you will be an astronaut one day and travel the galaxy for NASA or whatever you want to do. I feel like I barely know you but there is something about you that seems like we were meant to cross paths. Do you know what I mean?

I nodded my head vigorously, agreeing as I read the question. I wanted to tell her how madly in love I was with her, but she had her pop-influenced boy toy that I'm sure she wouldn't leave for me.

I really think you're cute and I'm embarrassed to say it out loud, this is why I have been trying to get you to say it, but for a smart guy you seem to lack the confidence to go for a girl that is clearly interested in you. Please write me back and let me know if you feel the same way too, or am I crazy? If I am, do not mention this to anyone, and never talk to me about it again.

–Venus

I was flabbergasted, frankly I didn't know what to say. But I picked up my pencil and wrote under her highly winded sentences:

What about Ronny? As if that was the only thing on my mind not that fact that she just confessed to liking me before I did. I had some bad conscience looming over my head, wondering if my ass would be kicked all up and down this school if

Ronny knew I stole his girl. I tapped her on the back and hand-ed her the note back.

Venus unfolded the paper and picked up her pencil and wrote back. She quietly slipped the note back over her shoulder and I unfolded it again.

What about him? I felt this would've been easier through text messaging but, number one, I didn't have her number, and number two, I felt like we were back in a time when people didn't have cellphones. It was kind of exciting.

Isn't he going to kick my ass when you tell him you like me? I wrote back.

He's got five other girls looking for the chance to be with him. He will get over it.

That must be nice. I wrote and handed her back the note. When she read it, she laughed out loud and Mr. Fletcher turned around from the board and called on Venus.

"What's so funny?" he said.

"Nothing, sir. I'm sorry."

"Well something had to be funny in order for you to laugh in the middle of my class."

"I'm sorry. I made her laugh, sir."

"Well I hope it was worth the afternoon in detention, Cil-lian." Mr. Fletcher could be a complete dick sometimes. I feel like he may have been an uber-dork in high school, kind of like me. He got his revenge on kids by being an asshole whenever he could.

"No. It's not all his fault," Venus said. I looked at her and shook my head. She looked back at me and mouthed, *"it's ok"*.

"Fine, then both of you have detention then." Venus looked at me and smiled.

After school we stood in front of the white board and wrote over and over, *I will not laugh in astronomy class.* We both had our own side of the white board that stretched across the whole length of the wall in front of the classroom. It felt weird being in the class this time of day with no one in the school, and no one in the classroom. It was so quiet I could almost hear my thoughts leaking out of my ears. I didn't know what I was going to say to her, especially after that note.

"I can't believe Mr. Fletcher made us go to detention for a little giggle," Venus said while writing in the black dry erase ink.

"He takes astronomy a little too seriously," I said. Venus laughed.

"You don't have to laugh at everything I say, you know." I glanced at her smiling back at me with rosy cheeks. I think we were flirting with each other. It was hard to tell because I didn't know I was capable of doing such a thing.

"I'm not fake laughing. I think you are funny. I already told you that."

"I don't see why, I just say what's on my mind."

"Your mind is funny then."

"If you had my mind you wouldn't think so." Venus laughed again and then stopped abruptly.

"Wait, you're not a serial killer are you?" She busted out in laughter at her own joke. Keeling over, one arm stretched across her belly and the other propped on her knee.

"Are you high?"

"No, but that would even be better being stuck in here. We could write I will not get high in class instead." Now I laughed. And the laughs from the both of us faded as we continued to write on the board.

"So about before. The note. I wanted you to know how I felt."

"Yeah." My heart rate increased heavily.

"What do you think?"

"I…Uh…" Why couldn't I just admit that I really liked this girl? What was I hiding from her?

"If you don't feel the same that is fine. I just thought maybe you felt that way too." She glanced at me, pulling her body away from the board and walking toward me. I stared at the board for a moment and cocked my head slowly as she inched closer to me.

"Venus, I can't tell you how ecstatic I am that you like me. I don't think you know how much I really want this." Venus scrunched her eyebrows and looked confused. "But…"

"But, what?" She said.

"I don't think I'm the guy you want to be with."

"How do you know what kind of guy I want to be with?" Venus was within arms distance now. I had capped my marker and put it on the ledge of the white board.

"I'm not very exciting. I don't play any instruments. I don't play sports, I don't have a ton of friends, and I've never had sex before." Venus looked down at the floor in disappointment. Then she looked back up at me with those green eyes, mixed like Saturn's rings. Her pupils grew and shrunk as she bit her lip.

"I hate sports, I don't play an instrument, and I'm not very exciting myself," she said, smiling at me. I felt this feeling inside me, like a match being lit. She wasn't going to give up until she had me. I never met anyone like this before, and I thought I was completely a fool for thinking that she would never even be interested in me. This whole time she had feelings for me, and I had no idea, just as she didn't know I had feeling for her.

She grabbed my hand and pulled me closer to her. There was this magnetism between us that I never felt before. It was like our energies complimented each other, there was static electricity binding us together. She pulled me closer until our lips touched and we kissed. Her hand grazed the back of my neck and I placed my hand on the small of her back. We pulled away from each other naturally and I opened my eyes and saw her face looking up at me.

"Am I dreaming right now?"

Venus laughed. "No, you're not dreaming."

"Good. Because earlier today I dreamt that you kissed me and when I woke, I was still sitting in that god forsaken desk."

"Oh my god, I know, right? Those desks are the worst," she said. "What are they, the same desks from 1980 or something?" I looked at her in wonderment.

"What?" she said with an inquisitive look. I just leaned in and kissed her again, cupping her face in both my hands.

"Best day ever," I said with my lips pressed against hers. Venus laughed and pushed me off her. She looked up at the clock. It was 4 p.m.

"It's time to get out of here," she said and grabbed her bag off the front desk motioning toward the door. "Let's go, lover boy."

"I like the sound of that." I grabbed my bag and followed her out the classroom door.

The Grocery Line

WHILE WAITING TO CHECK out at the grocery store, I listen to the conversations around me. While I wait for the cashier to finish with the person in front of me, I drift off into everyone else's lives around me. Almost every time I come to this store it is foreseen that the person in front of me is going to have some sort of problem with their items. A price check becomes a whole ordeal of involving the manager on duty, then the store manager, then they send the bagger to get a replacement of the item. It's like they know I'm in a hurry to get out of this place. I'll try to size up the person in front of me, measuring their abilities to have an issue, but who am I kidding? I never get that right. As my wife says, I'm a fuck up. Nothing I ever do is right, so here I am picking the slowest line as usual.

As I lay down the items out of my cart onto the automatic belt, I place down the plastic separator, so the cashier doesn't confuse my items with the person in front of me. I do whatever I can to avoid this problem considering it's the only one I really have control over.

I place the bananas, bag of apples, oranges, milk, coffee creamer, whole grain loaves of bread, packaged cheese slices, sliced turkey and ham for sandwiches, block of sharp cheddar cheese, wheat crackers, two steaks, two chicken cutlets pre-packaged in a Styrofoam bottom with shrink wrap, boxed whole wheat spaghetti, and spaghetti sauce in glass jars.

While I'm doing this, I hear the kids on the line next to me fighting over a candy bar as their mother yaps away on the phone about someone she saw on Instagram in a bikini that was obviously too fat to be posting on social media. The older woman in front of her finished and has had her groceries bagged by a dorky teenager named Cillian, but she can't figure out how the machine reads her debit card. I hear the clerk telling her to insert the chip, but she continues to explain that her chip doesn't work on the machine. She swipes the card, and the machine keeps beeping maniacally, basically yelling at her to insert the damn chip. I want to yell over the magazine rack *insert the god damn chip before all hell breaks loose and the demons ascend into this god forsaken grocery store.* But I hold my breath until she inserts the chip to appease the cashier whose name I don't know because their back is facing me. The payment is accepted, but before the woman walks away with her groceries in her cart, she tells the cashier that she's never used it before which is a complete lie, she just wanted to be difficult.

I wait behind the man in front of me. Of course, he had to get a price check on some organic celery. *Fucking seriously, dude!* I want to reach out and strangle this fucking John Cena wannabe! The well-nourished, physically fit man with a perfect full head of hair unlike mine. With my hands around his neck, I wanted to scream in his face, *"Knock off the organic food and stop working out! You're making me look like a tub of fat covered in hair! You're fucking it up for all of us average men out here!"* But I swallow that notion and clench my teeth together like I was swallowing vomit. I'm at the point where I just want this nightmare to end. I can feel my knees buckling and my chest getting tighter and tighter, like my torso has been wedged in between a vise grip slowly cranking tighter and tighter. I feel trapped like I feel in my marriage when my wife calls me a shit excuse of a man.

I feel so uncomfortable in this place with all these people around me. I need to get out of here as quickly as possible. It feels like everyone is working against me, that at any moment everyone is going to turn around and laugh at me, maybe Ashton Kutcher is going to pop out from behind the counter and tell me he's been following me around my whole life. I started nervously giggling to myself with the idea of my life being an episode of Punk'd.

I look up to finally see my groceries sliding across the scanner one at a time from the automatic belt, cycling the food down to the cashier. Jade was a rather young girl, probably still in high school. This could be the first job she ever had. She seemed to know what she was doing, bagging my food simultaneously. I think that this may be the quickest checkout I have ever encountered until it's time to check out and I reach into my pocket and realize I have left my wallet in the car. I panic and struggle to find that I had become one of them. One of the ever forgetful, overzealous, penny grubbing, asshole sucking, mother fucking dickholes that I had always complained about. I was the same as all the other douches that held up the line, a putz as my wife called it, a fucking putz because I forgot my wallet. I look Jade in the eyes and whisper that I forgot my wallet. She doesn't hear me, so I have to repeat myself louder. There are three people waiting behind me now. When I look back, the young girl right behind me rolls her eyes and the hipster fellow at the end of the line curses at me with an intense growl. I immediately cower down in front of the counter in hopes not to make eye contact with him. Jade tells me to pull off to the side of the store with the groceries and get my wallet. She hands me a receipt with a barcode at the bottom and motions me to the side. I run to my car to get my wallet and run back into the store. I pay for the groceries and place them all in the trunk of the car when my wife calls me. I pull my phone out of my pocket and answer.

"Did you get some organic celery?"

"Son of a bitch!"

Terms and Conditions

I HAD CAROLINE'S PHONE in my hand, reading the messages that she sent to some other dude through her Tinder app while she was in the bathroom. Probably something I shouldn't have done, but I kept wondering if she still used Tinder since we had been exclusively dating for a couple of months now. The tv remote was limply held in one hand while I scrolled through the text messages on her phone with the other. I immediately felt ill. Sick to my stomach to the point where I felt like I was going to barf up the Chinese food we ordered for our night together binge-watching Jessica Jones.

The things that this guy said to her, I had no idea she even liked that kind of behavior. *I'm gonna slurp yo' pussy up like a kitten drinking milk from a saucer.* What the fuck was I reading? Everything I saw made my heart palpitate in ways I'd never felt before. When she came out of my bathroom and discovered me holding her phone, I'm sure she felt the heat exuding from my body like I was a nuclear reactor ready to explode. She immediately questioned my actions and why I didn't trust her. Instead of diffusing the reactor for a cool down, she throttled the systems to high intensity by turning it on me, making me look like the bad guy.

The whole time she expressed what a paranoid fuck I was, I couldn't help but to think of how I wanted to bash her head in with the device I gripped so tightly. If I were the Hulk, it would have disintegrated. I continued to stand there as she pointed out the fact that we had met on the app, and that this is what society was like now. I couldn't understand how cold a person could be when five minutes ago we were cuddled up on this exact couch watching a TV show that we enjoyed together. I wanted to burn this couch now. I wanted to throw my TV out and never watch Jessica Jones again because it would make me relive this moment for the rest of my life.

How could I be so naïve to the fact that she had been doing this behind my back? My head was pounding, the blood rushing to my brain thumped in my ears like a drum line at a college football rally.

"Shut up!" I screamed. Her face went from offensive to defensive, fear spreading between her eyes. She stepped back toward the door.

Her pale face told me that my face had to be boiling red. The way she looked at me, her eyes diverting to my cheeks and my mouth as it foamed like Cujo made me realize that I had to dial myself back a bit. I realized I still held her phone in my sweaty palm.

"Get out." I wanted to slam the phone down, but I handed it to her instead. She grabbed it from me like it was her most prized possession and snatched her purse from the end table by the door and was gone so swiftly I barely had time to think about begging her to stay. I just wanted someone to spend my time with, someone that would appreciate being with me as much as I appreciated them, but I guess that was too much to ask. I turned off the TV. I turned off the lights. I turned off my phone, my computer, and my iPad and I went straight to the fridge where I had a bottle of whiskey waiting in the bottom freezer for such occasions as these. It was like I knew this was going to happen, or maybe I wished it upon myself—transmitting negative energy in the universe that slammed back with such force that it blasted me into a drunken coma. Weeks blurred together as one. The same routine daily: go to work hung over, deal with people and their problems, come home and get black-out drunk, continue vicious cycle.

I knew I couldn't handle the hang over anymore when one morning my boss pulled in the parking lot five minutes before we were supposed to open. The sun burned my eyes and my body felt like I had weights attached to my limbs. Georgi rolled up in his five-month-old Lexus IS 300-F-Sport, Ray-Ban sunglasses on, and an e-cig in his mouth. If you looked up douche bag in the dictionary, his picture was next to it. He got out of his car with this positive attitude that made me want to yak up the whiskey I had last night and the McDonald's egg McMuffin I had finished five minutes before he arrived.

"Are you ready to make some fucking money, bro?" Georgi said like we were friends, or wished we were.

"Yeah, man." I said, swallowing the vomit as it crept up my esophagus. Within the first hour we were open we had about twenty customers with every problem in the modern world of cellphone technology:

My phone won't send a text. My phone won't access Facebook. Why can't I get emails on my phone? Why is my bill so high? You told me I was getting a free phone, why am I paying for it on my bill? Why can't I delete all these tabs of porn in my web browser?

My skull felt like it was cracking in half. I couldn't take the complaining anymore. The pain struck my nerves and my heart felt shriveled up, enough to not give a shit about anyone that came through those doors. This one customer happened to be talking about Netflix with Georgi and he mentioned Watching *Marvel's Jessica Jones*. I immediately stopped applying a screen protector to a woman's phone and ran to the bathroom in the back office and threw up into the toilet. The sausage flavored whiskey burned all the way up my esophagus, projecting a mustardy liquid that splashed into the toilet and back out onto the floor where specs of puke-mixed toilet water hit me back in the face. I hurled some more knowing I was wearing the puke on my face now. The veins in my neck coursed thick blood to my face that made my head feel like it was going to erupt out the top of my skull like Mount Vesuvius. The worst was over, so I laid there on the disgusting bathroom floor, huddled next to the toilet, remnants of my breakfast and whiskey dribbling from my mouth down to my shirt. Georgi walked into the bathroom and saw me on the floor, looking like the life was drained out of me. The stench made him gag when he came within the vicinity of the toilet.

It took me a few weeks to clean up after that morning, and I had worked my way to being sober because I couldn't stand the smell, nor the taste of whiskey anymore. I had closed myself off from the world for months now. No going out with friends, no dates, and completely abandoning social media including apps like Tinder looking for a date. My head was clearer now that I stopped drinking myself into a black hole of misery. My friends, Mike and Chris, had been texting me for weeks trying to get me to go out with them, but I was clearly ignoring them, and they knew this.

I was in the middle of transferring this man's data to his new phone when Mike and Chris came in the store. Mike had a backwards Tampa Bay Rays hat on, and Chris just got some lines etched into his hair. I could tell they were ready to go somewhere with the way they were dressed, casual but nice. Normally they would come in with their work clothes on which consisted of being covered in paint and drywall dust.

"What's up, mother fucker!" Chris called out as soon as he saw me. My customer turned around looking shocked, but he didn't say anything.

"Dude, I'm working," I whispered back at him from behind the counter.

"Tone it down a minute," Mike said, slapping Chris in the chest at the same time. Chris rubbed his chest and made a displeased face.

"What are you doing tonight?" Mike said, placing his hands on the counter holding himself up.

"Just closing up and going home."

"You need to come out."

"No. I'm not going anywhere."

"Get over that bitch, bro," Chris shouted from the front of the store. My customer shook his head with disapproval at Chris' choice of language.

"Listen. We won't push you to do anything. You just need to get out and have a good time. It's been months since you've done anything."

"I wouldn't say anything," I said. My customer was looking over the computer screen as I tapped options on his screen to transfer data from his old device to the new one.

"Drinking at home by yourself isn't doing something. It's sad really," Mike said and looked at my customer. His old eyes looked back at Mike and back towards me. "What do you think?"

"Sounds pretty sad to me." He reserved any animosity towards me as Mike awkwardly included him into the conversation.

"See. Even this dude agrees."

"Can I talk to you for a minute?" I said to Mike. "It will be just a few minutes, sir. The data is transferring now." I pulled Mike to the side of the counter and Chris walked over to join in.

"Seriously, guys. I'm not going anywhere tonight," I whispered.

"Stop being a pussy," Chris whispered back. "You need to get out of this funk you are in."

"I am. I am out of the funk," I said. "I'm not ready to go out yet. It's not right yet."

"If you keep waiting for that right moment, you may miss a chance you never would have stumbled upon otherwise," Mike said. His positivity and well-mannered opinions always pushed me in the right direction before.

"I wouldn't know either way, so I think I'll be fine."

"Fine. Be a Debbie downer. I didn't think that you would turn into such a wuss from some whore that was cheating on you. Her loss, bro. Get on with your life."

"Don't let her win," my customer said. "Speaking from experience. I let a woman get the best of me and I wrote myself off and never met anyone I wanted to spend my life with. I regret every minute of it." Mike, Chris, and I all stared at the man in awe.

"Fuck yeah!" Chris said.

"Is my phone done transferring yet? This is some shit to wait here and listen to you being a pussy." Mike and Chris laughed.

"I like this guy. He's real as shit," Chris said.

"Alright, guys, that's enough." I walked over to my customer's phone and saw that the data was finished transferring. I unplugged the device and gave it to him. He scurried out in a rush and I closed the store.

NEXT THING I KNEW WE were catching an Uber to a club in Ybor City. When we got out of the car, the lights outside the club were blinding to me, brighter than I had ever seen them before—colors blended together. Mike and Chris pushed me into the club to deafening loud music, flashing lights gleaming among a sea of darkness. This kind of effect would cause an epileptic to have a seizure. All I saw was ghosting images of people's faces from the strobe lights. After a few minutes of squeezing through warm, sweaty bodies, my eyes acclimated to the flash bangs.

I remember seeing Chris's face, yelling something at me. His veins bulged in his neck and a level of frustration pulsed in his eye when I kept saying *"what"* which made him repeat himself. When he turned away from me and suddenly placed a bottle of beer in my hand, I understood what he said to me.

We stood by the bar on the first floor for a few minutes and sipped our drinks, scoping out the place. There was a group of girls dancing together in the middle of the dance floor. They wore slim dresses where the curves of their bodies were hugged tightly in shiny fabric. You could tell they had this night planned out. They weren't about to have a few dudes barge into their girls' night out. Without hesitation, Chris went up to one of the girls. His love for blondes made it clear which girl he was claiming. She was about six-foot-tall in her stilettos, could have been a model for all we knew, but Chris, at six-two, was taller than her. He grabbed her hands and began dancing. I was astonished that they didn't gang up on him like a pack of hungry gremlins. But Chris had a charismatic aura that let him do almost anything. I watched him dance with *Barbie*, talking into her ear. She looked up at him and smiled. I wish I knew what he said to her. Maybe I should try that move, but I'm sure it would land me in a jail cell.

The other girls began to look lonely while Barbie and Chris clung together like they were meant for each other. Mike shoved me, and I awkwardly tripped toward the girl in the blue dress. She looked frightened at first like she just avoided a collision. Her brown eyes pushed me away, her purse clenched under her arm, her eyes darted away and then locked eyes with me a second later. She was a shy girl, but there was something about her that I found soothing and attractive. Something came over me at that moment. I was tired of letting the moment slip away so I grabbed her hand and pulled her from the rest of her friends.

"My name's Carlos, what's yours?"

"My name's Meghan." She leaned into my ear and yelled over the loud music. I put my hand on her hips and she wrapped her arms around my neck. Her chestnut hair hovered over her eyebrows as colors of the rainbow from the dance floor's light show danced across it.

Song after song Meghan and I danced. We swayed to the rhythm and the beat, neither one of us knowing what we were doing. I looked at Meghan while the light shimmered in her eyes and I wanted to tell her that I just went through a weird breakup, but I didn't find it appropriate, nor would I be able to speak over the loud, bass thumping music in this place. It was nice to share moments with a person I'd never met before—hold her close—and be completely content with the situation. I felt comfortable being uncomfortable.

Time seemed to blend into a force of colors and muscle spasms. I think my drunkenness had been known amongst the girls and especially with Meghan, but she didn't say anything. She didn't say much at all, and neither did I. Barbie came over and grabbed Meghan's hand and they walked through the crowd of people. Meghan waved to me as she was dragged through bodies that soon consumed her and she was gone forever.

"Let's go up to the top floor. I want to see what it's like up there," Mike said. This club was the only club in Ybor that had a dance club on the roof outside. We climbed the metal steps to get to the roof. Chris opened the double doors to the rooftop where a live band played on a stage with laser lights streaming across the rooftop and zipping along the sides of the nearby buildings.

We stopped off at the first bar to the left to refill, not that I needed any more booze in me. But what the heck, I was celebrating my freedom and mourning the death of my relationship with Caroline.

"What did you think of that girl, Carlos?" Chris whacked me in the ribs with the back of his hand.

"Meghan?" I said with a condescending tone. "Did you get your girl's name?"

"Yeah, but I forgot it."

"That's nice," I said, unsurprised. "How am I going to get in touch with Meghan now?"

"Hey, man? We're not here to get you a girlfriend, we're here to have fun."

"Well I'm not having much fun right now. I can't just flash my smile at a girl and get her to sleep with me."

"I'm actually hurt that you think that's all I do."

"It's true, isn't it?"

"I just pick the ones that are probably dumber than me."

"That doesn't sound good at all," I said.

"Alright, guys. Enough talk," Mike said. He was like the all-powerful leader, always wrangling us up and controlling our childlike behavior. I agreed with Mike without having to say a word. I scanned the rooftop and enjoyed the ambiance.

The skyline was beautiful, buildings stretched into the sky, and the light from the streetlights below trailed up the sides with an orange gradient. I could faintly see some stars in the sky on this clear night. I inhaled deeply to capture this moment. Fresh air, music, and two friends I considered brothers surrounded me followed by hundreds of people on this beautiful night. Maybe it was the oxygen high I received from inhaling so deeply, but when I glanced at all the people, I kept seeing beautiful women having a good time. That's when I realized maybe I had been shut in my apartment for too long. There were plenty of fish in the sea and I needed to explore the waters more often. There was a girl standing in front of me that looked like a young Cameron Diaz but not as skinny. Our sloshed, unfocused eyes locked onto each other and I started to giggle for whatever reason. She laughed back, and for a second it seemed like we had our own inside joke. I wanted to say hello to her, but I felt this queasy feeling creep from my stomach up my esophagus. I held in some puke and swallowed it right away. I ran to the side of the building and puked. I watched my vomit rain down onto the street below, spewing out like a sewer drain into a cesspool, blood curdling screams echoed up the stacked brick wall, people pointed up to me—I felt bad, but I couldn't control myself, my stomach compressed like an empty bagpipe fresh out of air—struggling to make a note—I wheezed with a remorseful moan. My eyes felt like they would pop out at any moment. I couldn't breath and I felt like I was going to pass out at any second—probably falling off the building to my death, but the storm was over, I stopped vomiting and immediately felt the dizziness subside. The pressure that built up in my skull was like a balloon that was about to pop. My body completely drained of energy. I wanted to lie down, so I rested my cheek on the cool, brick ledge. I would sleep there for the rest of the night if I could. As my energy slowly came back, I lifted my head and looked down to see cops looking up at me, pointing, saying things that sounded like exasperated mumbo-jumbo.

Mike saw what had happened and he grabbed me from the ledge, strings of saliva dangling from my mouth. He pulled me by my shirt, half holding me up as he dragged me through the dance floor on the rooftop, signaling to Chris like we were running from a group of terrorists somewhere in the Middle East.

The police had sent a group up the fire escape to the top of the building. We exited the 2nd floor and saw two cops push their way through the dance floor with their flashlights gleaming into an ocean of sweaty, drunk people. They were shouting, "Move! Get out of the way."

Mike pulled me to the bar on the second floor and sat me on a stool. Chris stood behind me. I could see out of the corner of my eye that the two cops had made their way up the stairs, pushing people aside, moving towards the bar we were at. I looked over my shoulder where Chris had been standing, ordering another beer like nothing was happening. The cops were getting closer and I was getting nervous. The stench of puke was still prevalent and stinging my nostrils. I looked to Chris.

"Just stay calm." He turned to the bartender and grabbed the drink she placed on a coaster. The cops ran past us and made their way up to the third floor.

"They have no idea who did it," Mike said. "For all they know, your dumb ass is still up there."

After Chris slammed his shot of vodka, we bounced out of that place faster than you could say, *raining puke.*

When we exited the club, we turned down the street out in front of the place. People were walking on either side of the street. There were two girls standing on the corner that had felt the wrath of my vomit, talking to a police officer jotting it all onto a notepad. We went the opposite way, filing in between crowds of people outside the club. Now that my head felt lighter, I had some energy and I was super hungry and thirsty.

"Let's get something to eat." were the first words I said since my incident on the roof. There was a pizza parlor right up the block that had the best pizza in town. There was no better time to get a slice of pizza then after midnight at Gino's Pizzeria. Nothing had to be said. We all walked to Gino's down the block off the strip.

Gino's was like any typical Italian pizza parlor. The glowing sign above the doorway had the colors of the Italian flag embedded in the letters. The neon beer logos of Miller, Budweiser, and Yuengling all hung in the windows. I'd had enough alcoholic beverages at this point. I needed a tall glass of ice water and a cheesy slice of pizza to nurse me back to health. As we stepped in the building, Caroline was standing in line with a tall dude, her arms wrapped around his waist and they pecked each other on the lips repeatedly. *Why me.* This night couldn't have been any worse. I'd rather have been arrested by the cops than seen Caroline in my favorite pizza place in Ybor.

As soon as I walked in the door behind the guys, Caroline turned toward the door and saw me. Her eyes lit up and she ran over to me and gave me a hug. I didn't know what to do, I made eye contact with her model looking boy toy, and immediately felt a sinking awkwardness in my heart that felt like the Titanic sinking to the depths of the Atlantic. I didn't reciprocate the hug because I didn't know what he would do if I touched her, not like I cared really but it wasn't my place. I took one good sniff of her and immediately was transferred back to sharing Chinese takeout and watching Netflix at my apartment.

"How are you?" Caroline said with a drunken flair. She had been drinking too.

"Fine," I said. Caroline looked at me with a sour look on her face.

"Did you puke tonight?"

"Oh yeah, sorry." I held my hand up to my mouth.

"You must've had a fun night."

"Yeah, first time out since we..." I stopped myself from going any further.

"Wow. Okay. Didn't realize." She looked at me astonished that I hadn't moved on yet. I didn't want to talk anymore, and I sure didn't want to go down memory lane, so I looked to my right.

"You know Chris and Mike," I said to her, diverting another awkward conversation moment.

"Yeah." She gave a limp wave and smiled. "This is Phillip." She pulled the lanky, chiseled lug toward her, showing him off like the prized horse that he was; flaunting in my face that she was with a better looking, probably better lover, with better man genes than me.

"So, is this the guy that said he'd lick you like a kitten?" I said while watching her chin drop to the floor.

"What?" She was flabbergasted.

"You heard me," I said confidently back to her.

"What did he just say to you, babe?" Phillip looked down at the gaping hole in her face.

"I thought you would've been over that by now."

"I guess I wasn't then."

"What'd he say about a cat?" Phillip looked at me angrily.

"Shut up, Phillip." Caroline said.

"Listen, Phillip. I would be careful with this girl if I were you."

"Let's go." Caroline grabbed Phillip's hand and stormed towards the door.

"What is going on?" Phillip said, looking back towards me, confused and worried at the same time.

"Whoa! I can't believe you just did that," Chris said.

"Very cool, Carlos. I knew this night would make you feel better." Mike patted me on the back. Even after I said all that stuff to Caroline, I still felt like shit—physically and emotionally. It was our turn to order pizza, and I was starving.

"I'll have two cheese slices," I said to the guy behind the counter.

A week had gone by and I began to gain my courage back into my life. I was able to clear my mind and be happy with who I was and what I was doing in my life. While I worked on an upgrade for a customer's phone, Meghan walked in the store. I couldn't believe it was her. I immediately stopped what I was doing.

"What are you doing here?"

"Stacy told me that you worked here."

I didn't know who she was talking about for a moment and she must've guessed I was clueless to who Stacy was.

"My friend that had her tongue jammed down your friend Chris' throat."

"Oh yeah," I said. "Great to see you. Give me a few minutes and we can talk. okay? I'll take my lunch break."

"Take your time," Meghan said and took a seat on the bench by the front window. The excitement tingled through my body. Life handed me a new challenge and I accepted the terms and conditions for a new journey.

Teleport

THE TAMPA INTERNATIONAL Tele-Port was the number one teleportation terminal on the west coast of Florida. Anyone that came to Tampa Bay transported to this location. Billy Xander was doing the opposite. He was teleporting to work on teleporters in Beijing, China. Billy had worked his way up to being one of the head managing technicians on the construction of new teleport stations in China. There was a lot of crime going on in China with black market teleporters. Billy's job was to facilitate government regulated X-Porters and make sure they were operating according to international code. He was to go to China to code the X-Porters, so they would be un-hackable by criminals or terrorist organizations that used teleportation devices for their own agendas.

"Teleport 1105 is beginning commission. All travelers to Los Angeles, California please begin to board the teleporter's platform," a gentle A.I. woman's voice echoed through the Tele-Port wing. Billy eyed the attendants opening the hanger gate, scanning tickets while a line of people filed into the long hallway to their destination. Billy slicked his hand through his hair every time he was about to teleport. He was nervous for more reasons than one could count, but the fact that his friend Sanjay disappeared about a year ago during teleportation scared him. Sanjay didn't end up in Beijing where he was supposed to be, and no one had heard from him since his disappearance. Did he get lost in the transporting ether realm of no return? Or did he get hacked and re-routed somewhere criminals would exploit his expertise for their unknown causes? There was no telling, but Billy knew that Sanjay wasn't the only one he knew this had happened too. This line of profession was becoming more dangerous with every day he stayed in it.

"What the heck is taking so long? I got a meeting at 10:30 and if I'm late, I'm going to lose my job," the disgruntled man in front of Billy said. He rolled up his blazer sleeve and the hologram of his digital watch emitted into the air—*9:57am*. His beady eyes and disheveled, balding hair spoke to the fact that he didn't care much for looks. He turned to Billy for some accompanied banter about the Tele-Port service, but Billy looked at him with a great deal of disdain. "You know what I'm saying?" the man said. His cheeks were rosy and plump.

"Yeah, man, we all got places to be. Just relax, you will get there on time," Billy said, trying to focus on the device in his hand. The sheet of glass scrolled through a document with the movement of his eyes, speed reading through the schematics of the X-Porters his team was going to install.

"This place always has me running late." The man glanced down at Billy's device, trying to see what he was doing. Billy huffed, and thumbed down the privacy settings to blur out the content on the glass, now only visible to Billy's retinas.

"Maybe you should book the early transport instead of waiting till the last minute then," Billy said with his mouth cocked to the side in resentment. He didn't even want to have this conversation with an inconsiderate, time-traveling tele-porter, especially when he himself was having a small panic attack about transporting, but he hid his nervous jitter very well. The man grunted contemptuously and turned back around. Billy smiled, successfully irritating another human being by his rudeness.

All the people in the line to Los Angeles were now gone. The attendant touched the computer screen behind the counter and the Tele-Port screen read *Transport to Beijing, China 10 a.m.* A chime reverberated through the Tele-Port wing.

"Now boarding the Tele-Port for Beijing, China. Please have your tickets ready and all belongings with you for your trip. Thank you. Have a nice day."

"See, nothing to worry about," Billy said to the guy in front of him. He grunted again and continued forward to the loading bay. The attendant stood behind a small booth in front of the gate–she scanned the tickets from behind the blue glowing counter. The people in front of Billy handed her their tickets and walked down the long hallway to the teleportation bay.

Billy pulled out his ticket and handed it to the attendant. She observed him as she scanned the ticket, glancing down to the three-dimensional display of his face on the screen of her scanner. She looked back up to him.

"Welcome, William Xander. Enjoy your trip to Beijing," she said with a gleaming white smile.

"Thanks, Vivian." He looked at her name tag and directly addressed her. "But you can call me Billy." He darted his crystal-blues to her glistening ambers.

"Have a safe transport, Billy." She blushed as Billy's handsome smile glistened back at her. He winked at Vivian, almost forgetting about how nervous he was until he turned his head and looked down the long, sinuous hallway. Bright white LED rings hung from the ceiling evenly distributing light to the end of the hallway where he stopped behind the grumpy man right before the entrance of the teleportation bay. The hall felt claustrophobic, but through the open doors to the teleportation bay was an enormous room, the size of an airport hangar. Billy brought the device up to his mouth and spoke softly, "In teleporter now. Be there shortly." Then he hit send and immediately jammed the rectangular glass into his pocket.

A giant ring was held up by metal arms attached to a base bolted to the concrete floor. The blue energy emitted a bright sphere of electricity that looked like fire being sucked into a giant hole. There was a three second wait time for each person as they entered the teleporter. Colors and every fiber of existence of a living being disappeared—strung through a tight hole in the center of the ring, like thread through the eye of a needle.

Billy waited his turn, his palms sweaty, adjusting his tie, and taking baby steps forward. He thought of Sanjay as he stepped closer to the teleporter. Why was he thinking of him now? He should've taken his anti-anxiety medicine like he normally did, but he thought he would be able to handle it this time. Billy watched as the disgruntled man stepped into the blue haze and disappeared into the fraction of a dot in the middle of the sphere. It was his turn now. The technician stood at his podium with the controls to the destination and power to the device. There was a kill switch. If anything went wrong, the button would be pressed, and the portal would fold onto itself in an instant. The technician pulled up Billy's information on his screen.

"William Xander," the technician called out. Billy nodded at him. "Have a pleasant trip, hope to see you back again soon." Billy gulped and stepped into the blue sphere.

The intensity of colors stretched to infinity and flashed by like lightning. He felt like he was floating through water, unable to swim in any direction. The feeling of this moment lasted forever, like time had stopped. Billy couldn't see his physical form, just all the colors around him, swallowing him in this cylindrical vortex that seemed to be contorting and twisting everything around him. Nausea took effect, and Billy felt like he was going to throw up, but he couldn't go anywhere. He was propelled forward forever like the inertia of an object in motion without an outside force to disrupt the speed or direction. *How long am I going to be in this nightmare?* Nothing real, nothing solid, only bright colors stretching into oblivion. This was taking longer than normal—his anxiety was through the roof and moments in time kept flashing through the neurons of his mind. His childhood, his mother's face looking at him adoringly, and then a fit of anger from knocking over her vase, breaking into pieces. The crash of glass echoed forever through this tunnel of light. The crashing sound echoed so loudly it seemed to fold onto itself and break a barrier becoming just a single tinny sine wave.

Suddenly all he saw was blackness. Silence. Not a sound. Billy awoke in a room, bright and white. Nothing but his body lying on a table with his arms and legs strapped down. Billy angled his head and struggled to move his appendages but couldn't break free.

"Where am I?" he screamed out. His voice was dry and raspy. He was so thirsty. His arms and legs felt like he had competed in a triathlon. Overcome with exhaustion, Billy lifted his head again and pressed his chin to his chest to look down at the buckles holding his body down. He felt the prickle of hair from his face push into his naked chest.

There was a noise from across the room. A door opened, but there was only darkness outside the door. He heard steps faintly make their way to the doorway and then Sanjay appeared wearing a black suit.

"Sanjay?" Billy said, surprised. "Where have you been?" Sanjay looked at him plainly. No answer. Standing still across the room. "What's going on? Why do you have me strapped to this table like this?" Still no answer from Sanjay.

"Answer me!" Billy cried out. Sanjay moved closer to Billy. He walked up to the table and stroked his head. Billy tried to move his head where Sanjay couldn't touch him, but he couldn't escape so he stopped struggling. Sanjay stroked Billy's black hair, his expression devoid of all emotion, and backed up a step.

"I'm sorry we had to do this to you, Billy."

"What do you mean we?"

"Our organization. We need people like you," Sanjay said as if he was a robot.

"This is crazy. Let me go. I have work to do."

"Yes, you do have work to do for us now."

"Am I fucking dreaming right now? I thought you went missing a year ago."

"I did, but here I am. Doing the organization's work."

"Are you a slave or something now? Why are you talking like a fucking robot?"

"I am no robot, Billy. I have been converted to help the organization and fulfill their plans."

"Plans for what?" Billy said. "World domination?"

"You could say that."

"Let me out of here!" Billy screamed and kicked. "Let me out of here now!" The veins in his neck protruded and spit flew from his mouth.

"I'm sorry I cannot do that." Sanjay pulled a syringe out of his pocket and held it up in front of his face.

"What are you going to do with that?"

"You will see."

"Don't put that in me, Sanjay." Billy watched as Sanjay pressed upward on the syringe pushing the liquid through the needle. He slowly approached Billy.

"Don't do it. I'm begging you." Billy looked into Sanjay's eyes with a mournful stare. Sanjay grabbed his arm with his free hand and angled the needle towards Billy's vein pulsing from under his skin.

"If that's you inside, Sanjay, you won't do this," Billy pleaded. Sanjay stopped advancing and gave Billy a concerned look. It was the first sign of any emotion Billy saw in Sanjay's face during this whole interaction. "Just let me go and we can get out of here together." Sanjay continued to pause in thought. "We can stop this." Sanjay looked at the needle in his hand and appeared to be thinking about what he was about to do. Then he tightened his grip, pulled Billy's arm, and injected the needle's contents into his vein.

Billy screamed out, shedding a tear as his consciousness slipped and became fuzzy. Sanjay hovered over Billy's face—everything became a giant blur—his eyelids fluttered till he blacked out. Sanjay stepped back from Billy's comatose body and removed the syringe from the vein in his arm, placing it on the metal surgical table. He walked around Billy's body, examining his almost lifeless state. Sanjay brushed the hair from Billy's face and walked out the door into the blackness, closing the door behind him.

Blind Date

MY HANDS ARE CLAMMY, like a warm, moist towelette. I wipe my sweaty palms on my brand-new Dockers I bought last night, dampening my thighs. I spent the afternoon vigorously ironing out the crease where my pants hung from the knees, clipped to the Burlington hangers. I used the shoe polish kit on the faded leather of my fancy dress shoes I only wore on special occasions. My dad gave me this kit for my thirtieth birthday. It had been passed down through the generations like it was some sort of infamous family heirloom—I remember a tear building up in his eye when he reluctantly handed it to me wrapped in newspaper. My dad didn't cry all the years I known him. He didn't even cry when I graduated from college, but he shed a tear when he handed me that polish kit. I strapped on the nicest dress shirt I owned, brushed my teeth with whitening toothpaste, used mint mouthwash, and combed my hair for ten minutes trying to get it perfect.

I sat at a circular table for two, white cloth napkins folded into some pyramid shape and utensils on either side. The dimly lit restaurant made it hard to see the menu. My mind wasn't even focused on eating though. I couldn't think about what to order because I was so nervous about meeting this girl my married friends, Gary and Sara, set me up with. They said, "she's adorable and completely perfect for you." They were the kind of couple that finished each other's sentences. Sometimes it made me sick to be around them. They wanted to push their happiness on me, setting me up on blind dates. I hated blind dates and the last person they set me up with was a woman that loved to eat sardines on pizza, the smell was atrocious, and I'm not one to judge someone on their weight if we click, but she was a full hundred pounds heavier than me and we had nothing in common. She knew I was an iOS developer for applications, and she didn't even understand what iOS was. She had a damn iPhone in her purse. She pulled it out multiple times to text her friends while we had dinner, so how the fuck doesn't she know what iOS is? Ugh... beside the point, it felt like Greg and Sara were doing this to me on purpose and the worst part was, I kept going on these dates like they would lead to something.

Please don't think I'm crazy for doing the old-fashioned blind date thing. I know what you're thinking, why not use dating apps? Glad you suggested that. Actually, I've used just about every dating app out there, especially since most of them are designed by friends of mine. These apps are the worst. No one is who they say they are, and most of the time I get stood up. I've been catfished by a few that made me want to quit dating all together. Sometimes I think I'm doomed to be alone forever. Either I'm too picky with women, or the women I'm dating tear me apart like they were expecting a dinner date with Dwayne Johnson or John Cena. When they see me: the curly hair, nerdy classes, and skinny physique they almost turn around running like they were expecting a hunk of man meat that they could brag to their friends about how great the sex was.

I can feel my airways closing. I begin to hyperventilate so I take a puff of my inhaler and try to quiet my mind–push every thought out and focus on listening to the soft classical music playing in the restaurant. The other folks in here quietly eat and talk to each other with a whisper like everything they're saying is a secret. It felt like I was going to be executed in this place, maybe I was meeting an assassin that would finally put me out of my misery, but that couldn't be further from the truth. A guy can wish, right?

The waiter came to my table, his nose in the air, small mustache above his lip like he was Clark Gable from *Gone with The Wind* or just a French snob. A white towel hung from his arm bent at the elbow while he bowed forward and spoke softly so no one else would hear.

"Is the other member of your party showing up, sir?" he said with a hint of sarcasm in his voice. It was like he knew why I was sitting by myself in this posh restaurant. I wanted to turn to him and tell him to fuck off, but that wouldn't be the best decision I've made especially if my date showed up and saw my rude behavior.

"Yes, she should be here any minute now."

"Would you like anything while you wait, sir?"

"Cheapest glass of wine, please." I might as well get a little buzz while I waited. Maybe it would loosen me up instead of being the typical clenched asshole I was when it came to meeting women.

"Sure thing, sir. Cheapest glass of wine. As you wish." He repeated louder so that others in the restaurant would hear. I wanted to slap him in the head at that moment but held myself back.

After he walked away, a woman in a black blouse and grey tight jeans walked through the door. Her chocolate hair was pulled in a bun and black rimmed glasses made her crimson red lips pop while matching her high heels. She came to my table and looked directly in my eyes, big brown-saucers staring at me. She had a slight resemblance of Zoe Saldana and for a second all I could think of was Gamora from *Guardians of the Galaxy*. Maybe for Halloween she could paint herself green and I could be Peter Quill. She raised her eyebrows in question as I plummeted back to Earth.

"Harold, right?" she said, her hand on the chair opposite of mine. I cleared my throat.

"Yes... yes... please sit down." I half got up to help her into her chair like a true gentleman would, but she was already pulling the chair out, plopping in the very thinly padded seat, then continuing to tuck her purse under the table at her feet.

"I'm Aubrey, nice to meet you." She reached her hand over the table. I followed her lead and shook her hand, hoping my clammy hand wouldn't gross her out.

"Hi, Aubrey, Harold, or most people call me Harry."

"A little nervous, are you?" She raised her half-cocked smile as if she could see right through me.

"Just a little. Not the first blind date I've been on, usually they don't go so well." I gave away too much information. I had to shut myself up.

"Yeah, I know. Same here. The idea is just absolute blasphemy, but this is what we do right?" She said with a lighthearted giggle as the words left her mouth. I was astounded by her and perplexed at the same time.

"You're a little strange, aren't you?" she said, squinting her eyes at me. The candlelight in the middle of the table gleamed in the reflection of her eyes.

"Well, I'm... uh, a little different I guess...just a little shocked... really."

"Shocked? About what?"

"How incredibly beautiful you are. I really wasn't expecting much since Greg and Sara usually fix me up with..."

"A snoozer!" she interrupted me. My face felt like it was bright red, but thanks to the dim lights I didn't think she could notice.

"You could say that." I laughed.

"They aren't the best matchmakers. At least not as much as they say they are," she said, eyeing the waiter as he returned with my wine.

"Your cheap glass of wine, sir." His nose shot in the air like the snooty bastard he was.

"That actually sounds really good to me, may I have a glass, please?" Aubrey looked at the waiter. She held her chin like she was the thinker statue. "This place is overpriced anyways," she said, looking back to me with a huge smile, winking.

I laughed and covered my mouth immediately. The waiter left the bottle on the table and Aubrey watched him walk to the kitchen to get another glass. She grabbed the bottle and took a swig as soon as he entered the kitchen door. She smacked her lips together a few times.

"Not bad. You have good taste." She laughed as my eyes opened wide in disbelief. I don't know what it was, but this girl was amazingly entertaining to me and I really liked her sense of style. I would never dream of doing what she just did in a fancy restaurant like this. I couldn't help but smile at her.

"You know, I don't know why Greg and Sara pick places like this. Do they think a fancy restaurant is going to add to the romance of going on a blind date?"

"I often wonder the same thing, and Greg always comes up to me the next day, jamming his elbow in my side like, how did it go? Did you get any?"

"Sara does the same thing except she asks if I gave him head!" She chuckles.

"Are you serious?" I felt completely awkward, and I couldn't help but thinking, *"Do women just go around giving head on blind dates?"*

"Yeah. It's ridiculous. I think they live vicariously through us single people, not realizing what a nightmare it is."

"I agree. Just because they met in a fancy restaurant doesn't mean the whole world does the same." I think Aubrey could tell I was looking at her weirdly since she said the thing about giving head. She leaned over the table and said in a quieter voice,

"And I asked Sara. She doesn't give head, but she immediately thinks that's the first thing I do because I got these big juicy lips." She pointed to her lips and took another swig from the bottle. "But don't tell her I don't give head, especially on the first date."

"My lips are sealed." I backed up and did that stupid zipper motion, throwing the zipper away and all, like a complete putz. She thought it was funny though.

"You know what? Let's get out of this place. I could go for a slice of pizza and a beer." She got up from her seat, sipping from the bottle and then placing it down on the table.

"Now you're talking my language." I got up and grabbed my jacket from the back of the seat. As she walked away, I threw a twenty on the table for the wine. Hopefully that would cover it.

WE WALKED OUT THE RESTAURANT and headed down the street to the little pizza shop called Mom and Pops. I know, I know, pretty generic, but it was owned by Mom and Pop Gambino, who moved here from Italy to start their own pizza joint. Why not New York? Well, they hated the weather there and there's a dime a dozen pizza places, they wouldn't survive the competition.

"So, what do you do?" I asked Aubrey, my hands in my pockets, not quite sure of how to open a conversation while we awkwardly walked in silence to get pizza.

"I'm a financial advisor, blah, blah, blah. Pretty boring. I heard you design apps and software programs," Aubrey said, pulling her purse up over her shoulder.

"Yeah, I do. Not too fun either."

"Adulting sucks, doesn't it?"

"From time to time."

"I'm glad you're not a serial rapist."

"Where did that come from?"

"Eh... Let's just say one of the guys Sara and Greg fixed me up with was a serial rapist. They didn't know and neither did I, but I got this rape-y vibe because he would lick his lips every time I caught him staring at my breasts. Really creepy."

"That sounds like a really weird date. I had one that talked about sucking toes. I was like check, please." I held my finger in the air and Aubrey laughed!

"That is one crazy bitch. Talking about licking toes on the first date."

"I guess the girl knew what she wanted from the get-go. I wasn't that guy though."

"You're funny." Aubrey grinned, her shoulders slightly lifting in a cute shrug. There was this nervous tick in my chest, but it seemed to calm as her brown eyes locked with mine.

"Really? I am usually not very funny." Some cars drove by us while we walked on the sidewalk. I watched a few teenagers drive by with music blasting in their vehicle.

"Well, I think you are."

"I think you're funny too. This is the most fun I've had on a date that Sara and Greg set up and it's only the first thirty minutes." I looked down at my watch.

"You know what they say about the first thirty minutes?"

"No. What?"

"I don't know. Thought I was making up something great for a second. If there was, I would say..." Aubrey reached in the back of her mind, but I could tell she already knew what she was going to say, she just needed to give herself permission to say it.

"You could tell within the first thirty minutes that was someone you could spend the rest of your life with." Aubrey scratched her head while the words came out as her confidence faded with the fear that I would run to a cab right now.

"Wow, that is super romantic. I don't think I would've thought of that one," I said, congratulating her on her romantic efforts.

"Thank you, thank you. I would like to dedicate this award to..." Aubrey took a bow and clasped her hands together. I couldn't help but to laugh. This girl was hilarious. I had never met anyone like this before, especially on a blind date. My heart skipped a few beats like it was frolicking through the meadow, excited and full of glee.

We arrived at Mom and Pop's and I opened the door like a real gentleman this time.

"You don't have to play this gentleman trick with me you know."

"It's okay, I wanted to."

"Alright, I'll let it slide this time but next time I won't be so nice," she said, as I followed behind.

After we sat down, we sipped some beer and took a few bites of our pizzas. We engaged like we had been together for years.

"This pizza is so good," Aubrey said with her mouth half full. I smirked at her, finishing up my previous bite.

"I think it's a rule that you're not allowed to talk with your mouth full on the first date," I said with a chuckle, grabbing a napkin and wiping the grease from my lips.

"So un-lady like of me, I know. Always been a problem of mine." She chewed, blocking her mouth with her hand. She washed her food down with a swig of beer.

"What was the best date you ever been on?" I asked inquisitively. I wanted to know, but I wasn't sure how I was going to take the news if she gave me details like, this six-foot four, burly man that built houses or something like that. To me, Aubrey looked like she had guys knocking down the door to be with her, so I was perplexed why she would be single for so long. We all know why I'm single, but for her, what was up?

"Honestly, this is the best date I've been on." Aubrey leaned over the table and whispered close to me.

"Aww, that was sweet," I said sarcastically. I wasn't buying it. My eyes squinted, staring at her looking for a sign of a joke somewhere. But she leaned back and looked at me blankly.

"I'm serious. Almost every time I go out with a man, I feel like I got to be this perfect woman, the woman they've been looking for their whole life. And when I meet them, within the first five seconds I can tell how things are going to go at the way they look at me."

"Really?"

"Yeah. No one has ever looked at me the way you looked at me tonight." I didn't know if that was a good thing, or a bad thing, but I was banking on it being good for me. "Usually I get the look like oh no, my mom's not gonna like this bitch. Or I hope she puts out."

"You can tell from the first five seconds if someone's thinking that or not?"

"Believe it or not," she said with a smirk on her face.

"What did I look like to you?"

"I don't know how to describe it, but you looked at me like, she's the most beautiful woman I've ever seen, and I hope I don't fuck this up."

"Wow! I gotta hand it to you. That was spot on."

"I told you I could read a guy pretty damn good." Aubrey cocked her head, gloating in her ego.

I looked down at my half-eaten pizza and couldn't help but to wonder if she had tried the dating apps as well. I mean who hasn't that is single, right?

"Were you ever on Tinder or anything like that?"

"Are you kidding me?" she said sarcastically. "Who hasn't these days? The real sad thing is there are married people on that app looking for quick one-night stands. I figure those creeps out quick too. I can tell a married man within the first five seconds of seeing him. Nervous sweaty look on his face. Scanning the room to see if he knows anyone, who might be watching him. You think these guys were being followed by the F.B.I. Shitting your pants kinda look. I almost pegged you for one of them at first, but it was a completely different look when I got closer."

"What do you do when you peg them?"

"I usually go running for the door before they see me coming. I don't want to get caught up in that drama."

"I don't want to sound rude, but what attracted you to those apps?"

"Have you used it before?"

"Yeah. It wasn't my thing."

"Same here. One thing I noticed about dating and being a woman, there are a lot of creeps out there just looking to bump uglies and I get that, but that isn't me either."

I nodded my head because it made so much sense to me. Here we were surrounded by strangers, always trying to find other strangers to mingle with, but there's always that one person you click with, and they are out there somewhere, you just have to find them. I folded my pizza in half and took another bite, chewing slowly as I took in the atmosphere—the feeling of relief that I wasn't alone in the world. I sipped my beer to wash the pizza down and leaned back.

"What do you want to do now?"

"Want to see a movie?"

"I guess. What did you have in mind?"

"We will see when we get there. Doesn't really matter to me. I just want to sit next to you in a dark room and see something on a big screen."

Things were going so smoothly. It was like my prayers were finally answered. Aubrey really seemed into me, but I couldn't help but wonder if it was all a hoax. Nothing went this smoothly for me. This had to be some game I was playing. Either she was telling me everything I wanted to hear, so she could mark another peg on her list, or this was as real as it got. Why did I have to think that way, why couldn't I just enjoy this moment without thinking there was some sort of catch?

We left Mom and Pop's and grabbed an Uber to the nearest cinema, which wasn't the nicest theater, but it would do. When we arrived, we hopped out of the car and headed inside the theater. The billboard outside displayed the movies playing that night surrounded in old fashioned lightbulbs, which happened to have a few blown out around the border of the sign. It had an old-timey cinema vibe from the years before digital film, amazing Dolby audio, and crazy 3D gimmicks took over the theater chains. "Which one is playing right now?" Aubrey asked the clerk behind the counter. "Red Ring Rising. Previews just started." The clerk was a pimpled face nineteen-year-old that seemed bored that he was alive right now.

"What the hell is that about?" I said, furrowing my eyebrows in question.

"It doesn't matter. We will see it." Aubrey said to the clerk.

"That will be ten dollars."

"Here's a twenty, get me some popcorn please."

"You want butter on that?"

"Uh...yeah!" Aubrey said with a dumbfounded look on her face. She looked at me and whispered, "Who doesn't get butter on their popcorn at the movie theaters?"

"I'm sure there's some people. Like Greg and Sara," I whispered back to her. Aubrey threw her head back and laughed.

"You are so right." She cackled away. Pimple face looked at Aubrey, confused. He must've thought she was laughing at him.

"Two Sprites, too," She barked at him after he turned around with a scoop of popcorn in his hand.

"Yes, ma'am," he said and went back to scooping the popcorn into the large bag.

"What if I wanted a Coke?" I said, just kidding around.

"I'm paying, you get what I say you get." Aubrey cackled again. "If you want a Coke, get one."

"I was just playing. Sprite is fine. I don't need caffeine this late anyways."

"Me neither." I realized how old we sounded, but what could I say, my body was sensitive to caffeine at night.

We stood at the glass case that doubled as a counter, filled with shitty candy I used to eat as a kid that would no doubt give me cavities by tomorrow as an adult. The Sour Patch Kids, Snow Caps, humongous Crunch bars, chocolate covered cookie dough, and of course, my favorite, Rolos—the caramel filled chocolate that would stick to my teeth so badly I would have to use my fingers to pry the glue-like substance from my molars before my mouth cemented shut.

Pimples handed over the popcorn and drinks. We walked down a long, creepy hallway that smelled like feet. The buzzing fluorescent lights flickered, and I felt like we were about to step into a fun house or the Twilight Zone, but we pushed through the double doors to one of the smallest theaters I've ever been in. Couldn't have been more than thirty seats in the theater and the floor had a slight angle descending to the front row that was no farther than ten feet from the screen. I imagined that people that sat in those seats would have neck aches for the next week. I followed Aubrey as she picked the middle row seats on the left side of the theater.

"So, you're a lefty?" Aubrey looked baffled and confused at first but got the joke in a couple seconds.

"No, I'm a righty. Just thought this was a good seat."

"It's a fine seat."

"You have a lot of complaints."

"That's why they call me the complainer."

"Well we're going to have to fix that," Aubrey said, shoveling popcorn into her mouth. I watched her for a moment, kind of awkwardly—to the point where she felt me watching her and turned to me with an inquisitive look, like she thought she had something on her face.

"What?"

"I'm...really enjoying this night."

"Me too."

"I hope this is real." My mind let my mouth open and let the words fall out uncontrollably.

"What do you mean? Of course, this is real." Aubrey looked confused. I stammered for a second because I didn't know what I was going to say, or how I was going to explain how I felt.

"Is there something wrong?" Aubrey said, putting the bag of popcorn in her lap as the projector changed to another preview.

"No," I whispered, leaning towards her.

"What the hell are you whispering for? There's no one in here."

"Sorry, I just thought this was an embarrassing conversation I didn't want anyone to hear if they did walk in."

"Get to the point, Harry." Aubrey looked at me like she was about to strangle me.

"I feel like this is too good to be true though. Don't you?"

"No. I don't. I think we both deserve this. We're having a good time, aren't we?"

"Yeah, I am, but that's the thing. I never have a great time on dates. Especially a blind date."

"I don't get it. What are you saying?"

"Ima...Ju...Just forget it," I said and tried to grab some popcorn out of the bag resting in her lap, but she pulled it away.

"Tell me now," she said with her eyes popping out of her skull. If she started foaming from the mouth right now, I would completely understand her rabid tendencies. I envisioned her biting into my neck and ripping my jugular, blood gurgling all over the theater floor.

"I almost feel like you are playing me, and someone put you up to this," I said, squinting my eyes as if she was about to take that lethal bite.

"Are you kidding me right now?"

"Well the way you're acting, I'm guessing I was completely wrong."

"You must be some kind of idiot. Why the hell would you think I was playing you?"

"It just crossed my mind because it's happened to me before."

"What am I supposed to do? Just pretend you didn't say anything now? How did you think this was going to play out for you in that stupid man brain of yours?"

"It just came out," I said. "I didn't want to say it."

"But you were thinking it." She looked at me and I could see her heart sink to her stomach from the way her eyes flooded with frightening realization. "When did you first feel like this?"

I winced and fumbled around for a few seconds.

"How long?"

"Pretty much since we first met."

"Wow. You are a dick." She dumped the bag of popcorn over my head and walked past me sitting in the row among an empty theater as the movie started.

"You were the first one I was wrong about." She looked back at me from the aisle and walked out the double doors. The light from the hallway crept into the theater and flooded the screen where the opening sequence of the film had started.

I brushed the popcorn off my head and tried to avoid stomping on the popcorn, smashing it into the already filthy carpet. I ran through the double doors and chased after her down the hallway, through the lobby where pimples had been cleaning the popcorn machine. I shouted at Aubrey as she walked out the glass doors. She stood outside in front of the empty parking lot of the theater. I watched her for a moment and crept out the door to stand next to her.

"I'm sorry, Aubrey. I didn't mean it that way," I said trying to come up with some shitty excuse for her not to leave right now. She was crying and wouldn't face me.

"What do you mean then?" She said, sobbing into her hands. "That I am some whore hired to make you feel good about yourself?" she said, spinning around, her mascara dripping down her cheeks.

"I can't believe you." The level of humiliation was written on her face in black ink. "I thought I found the guy for me! All the signs were there. You weren't a creeper, you weren't married. You were funny, and you were cute." She wiped the tears from her eyes, smearing the mascara across her cheeks.

"I'm sorry. I wish I could take it back. Believe me."

"Everything I had done to prepare myself for a man I wanted to spend my time with proved me completely wrong. I feel like such an idiot right now."

"Don't feel like an idiot," I said, moving closer to her. I came within inches but kept my distance in fear I would make things worse if I touched her. "If anyone's an idiot, it's me."

"Yeah, you are," Aubrey said, sniffling.

"I know. I have this complex that if things are too good to be true, they might be."

"Sounds like you have some issues."

"I do. I admit it. But the reason I'm that way is because Greg had done that to me before. He set me up with this girl in college that happened to like me so much, and she seemed like a girl of my dreams. I was never good with girls. I always said the wrong thing at the wrong time, as you can see. Greg paid that girl to spend time with me and made me feel like I had a shot with her. It's just something I haven't gotten over."

"Wow. That is one shitty friend. I thought Sara was bad."

"Yeah. They really deserve each other, don't they?"

"They do."

"Don't ask me why I still hang out with him. I guess just like the women in my life, I never really had many friends either." Aubrey sniffed some air and pulled a tissue out of her purse. She wiped her eyes and her nose and put the tissue back in her purse.

"I'm sorry that you had to deal with that." Aubrey said and her glazed eyes were determined on a decision she had made when she walked out that door. "It was nice meeting you tonight and I did have fun, but I must be going now."

"No Aubrey please don't," I wasn't able to finish the sentence because I knew she was right. It was a fun night and I had let my past get in the way of something that could have been great. She smiled at me and stepped off the curb when an Uber pulled up. I slightly waved at her as she got into the vehicle and drove away. Maybe this is the way it was meant to be. This is the last time I go on a blind date and the last time I let my judgments get in the way of my emotions. Aubrey deserved better than me second guessing her motives. She deserves happiness and hopefully one day I will see what that looks like too.

Twin Lakes

CYNTHIA PERDUE WAS bound and gagged, lying on the deck of the cabin inside a small boat. She felt the rattle of the floorboards as water smacked against the hull. She leaned her head to the side, coming to the realization of a terrible throbbing headache with a distinct burning sensation in her sinuses. The moonlight peeked through the clouds and lit the boat on the lake. The summer thunderstorm had just let up and the rain had leaked into the cabin from the deck. Heat lightning flashed through the clouds—sparks of light flashed through the dark cabin. Cynthia pulled her tired bones up into an upright position and leaned up against the side of a bench. She heard someone whistling; a short, tone-deaf whistle that she didn't recognize.

Cynthia knew she had to be on the lake, but how did she get here? Who took her here and why were her wrists and ankles bound with duct tape? The tiny hairs on her arms tugged from the adhesive when she moved, and her extremities felt numb from lack of circulation.

Clunky thuds of boot soles crept towards her side of the boat until a man's silhouette stood in the cabin doorway. Moonlight engulfed the man's broad shoulders. Cynthia cocked her head and in a single motion, swung her legs from under her and spun on her butt like a top, facing the shadowed man.

"What do you want from me?" she screamed. The moon blinded her sensitive eyes and blackness shrouded his face. Like a mute, he was silent, but his boots did the talking for him. Each thud made Cynthia tremble with fear of what was going to happen next. Tears trickled down her face. He hunched over and softly held her chin in his hand. She looked up and saw him grinning back at her. His heavy hand landed on her face, forcing her body to crash to the floor with a smack. He grabbed Cynthia from behind and flipped her over, proceeding to pick her up and then toss her limp body down on the cushioned bench. He grasped at her pants and yanked them down with such force her hips pulsated with pain.

"No! Please! No!" Cynthia begged while she squirmed. He put most of his weight to hold her head down, while his other hand held her back. Cynthia felt like he was crushing her skull while his rough hand gripped her spine like a vise. She cried when he forcefully inserted himself into her, pumping hard and fast. Cynthia screamed with every movement. He took his hand from her skull and slid it down to her neck and squeezed tighter, and tighter. Cynthia's cries for help turned to gasps as her air was cut off. Sight and sound faded as she felt herself blacking out. The constant motion of being shoved into the plastic leather was like the waves knocking up against the boat. Her eyes rolled into the back of her head bulging like they would pop any moment. Saliva drooped from her mouth as she faded into the blackness of her mind to the thudding of bare flesh slapping together.

A PHONE CALL CAME INTO the sheriff's office, reporting another body in the lake, the second one in a week. Five bodies have been found in the lakes within the last month alone and they were all women and girls visiting from out of town.

Detective Donald Granger rolled over in his twin bed and answered the annoying buzz of the phone vibrating on the nightstand inside an empty room. He planted his feet on the floor with an exhausted sigh while lifting the box of cigarettes. He engaged with the cigarette like it was the only thing that understood his every need. He drew in a breath of smoke, breathing life into him like he drank a pot of coffee. The smoke left a haze in the empty, dimly lit room while he paced across the floor, stumbling to find clean clothes to wear.

Cynthia's body was found by a local walking his dog early that morning. Donald arrived at nine a.m. sharp with a coffee in hand, and his navy-blue tie loosely slung around his neck. His five o'clock shadow was early and if he let his facial hair grow more than a day, he was on his way to becoming a hippy. He made his way down to the crime scene where he saw Sheriff Holden standing behind the yellow caution tape. The sheriff was speaking to one of the forensic scientists when he stretched his neck out, watching Don duck under the tape.

"Hey, Don," Sheriff Holden called out. A couple deputies stood nearby and the forensic scientist snapped a few photos of the body that had washed up on the shore. Don held his hand over his face to block the sun glistening off the lake.

"Mike." He nodded his head at the Sheriff. "So, what do we have here? Another strangulation dumped into the lake?"

"Yeah. Same as last one."

"So why don't you have someone patrolling the lakes at night to catch this fucker?"

"You know why, Don."

"Yeah, yeah, yeah. Spare me the money talk."

"Listen, you know this by now. I run the office and my deputies. You come in whenever we need a case solved." Sheriff Michael Holden's mustache furrowed. "You chose your way, I chose mine."

"Ok, Mike, I get it. I'll do my job and you do yours." He walked to the body of the bloated, young girl that was a blueish green color. "How old is she?" Don sipped from his coffee cup.

"Her driver's license was wedged into her pocket like the others. She turned 18 last week. Must've been up here celebrating her birthday."

"Any family members report her missing yet?"

"No."

"Friends?"

"No. It's probably too early for them to notice she's gone."

"Let's find out where she was staying and get someone down here to ID the body."

Don knelt to one knee and eyed Cynthia's throat. Thick, finger-like bruises surrounded her neck, her expression was flat and painless. Her wet, brown hair was tangled and covered with sand from the shore. Her lips were thin and skin color faded. Don pulled her driver's license and looked at the lively photo of her weeks prior. Her birthday was February 12th 2,001. His eyes diverted toward her wrists where bruises and a sticky residue were left on her skin. He glanced at her bare ankles which looked the same. He pulled a pen from his pocket and proceeded to lift her shirt. Most of the girls found were raped, murdered, and thrown in the water like trash. The water washed away any evidence of DNA from the suspect and with the bodies fully submerged in water sometimes for days or weeks at a time, it was hard to find any fingerprints. Don knew that the suspect was smart. He used condoms, and gloves to keep fingerprints off the body. This one was different though. The body was fresher than the last few. She may have been in the water for eight to ten hours at the most. Don noticed she was naked from the waste down and spotted something sticking out of her swollen vagina.

"Forensics, get over here." The dorky looking forensics specialist ran over with gloves on and a small box with a clamp on the front. Don looked at what looked to be a tackle box. "You go-in fishing?"

"No, sir." The forensics specialist had his badge pinned to the lapel of his shirt. Chad Reinhardt. "Chad, give me some gloves and a baggy."

"Right away, sir." Chad fumbled with the box and rifled through the compartments to pull out some gloves and a plastic bag.

"First time?" Don said to Chad, leaning over the girl's body, waiting with his hand held out impatiently.

"No, sir."

"Stop with this sir shit. Call me Detective Granger or Don."

"Yes, sir... I mean, Detective Granger." Chad handed over the gloves and the bag.

"There you go." Don said with a condescending tone. He then reached down and pinched his fingers together and pulled out the remnants of a broken condom and dangled it in front of his face. There was some semen left in the pouch of the condom tip. He slid it into the bag, "I got you," Don said as he zipped the bag closed.

Don handed the bag to Chad and began to pull his gloves off. "Analyze that at the lab and let me know what you get. Cross reference any records you find with any history of convicted rapists and/or molesters in the system, from Tallahassee to Miami," Don snapped the latex gloves off his fingers, rolled them into a ball, and forced them into his pants pocket.

"That's probably thousands of people, si...Detective Granger."

"Probably, but there's probably one that will match the description we're looking for if he's in the database."

"Ok. I'm on it." Chad packed his things and the evidence bag in the utility box and walked off the shore to his vehicle parked across the street.

Mike saw Chad walk off scene, so he made his way back to Don who was hovering over the girl.

"You find something? He left in a hurry." Mike's mustache danced with every word.

"Yeah. I think this guy just made a huge mistake, either he's being sloppy and thinks he's getting away with something, or he planted enough evidence on her to give us a clue to who he is."

"Why would he do that?"

"Every serial murderer wants to be found, Michael. They crave it. They want notoriety for their work like any other profession. The difference is, he's playing with these young girls' lives and I'm not going to stand by and watch him do it."

DON DROVE AROUND TOWN asking if anyone saw anything suspicious on the lake last night. But, like usual, the locals never noticed anything. They go to bed early, especially this time of season because all the kids are out making a ruckus. It was the only way to avoid the confrontation with drunken people wandering their town.

Sam Wentworth said that most the kids in the area go to a couple bars and drink. He caught a couple having sex out back on his dock one night. He heard noise from out back and threw on the flood lights to catch the culprits in mid-act. He didn't report anything because he didn't want to get them in trouble. Sam remembered being young and getting into trouble himself, but he advised Don to go to the Twin Lakes Saloon because it was closest to the lake and where some underage drinking went on.

Don parked outside the bar waiting for people to pack in the place. It was after 10 p.m. and that was when the traffic began to flow like Sam said. Don watched from his inconspicuous spot at the end of the parking lot under a tree in the dark. He was going incognito to blend in the crowd. He strode through the parking lot with blue jeans and a white t-shirt under a leather jacket. He pulled the Tampa Bay Rays cap down just above his eyebrows to shade his face. Out front of the bar, the Twin Lakes Saloon was missing an 'O' which looked like it said Salon. It was on Main Street about three quarters of a mile from the lakes. The closest bar to the water—most of the times the *kids,* as Don would call them, would go down to the lakes drunk after the bar closed and go skinny dipping, especially around spring break. Occasionally a high school kid would mix in with the bunch and get drunk with their college friends or chalk their IDs to make them seem older. Twin Lakes Saloon was known for slipping up on ID checks. The owner, Harry Watkins, wouldn't turn down a buck when it was handed to him. He was a scummy, bald mother fucker, as Don would put it. But he hadn't been caught selling alcohol to a minor yet.

Don stepped into the establishment and grabbed a seat at the bar among a sea of young faces, crowded with smoke and the smell of old, sticky beer. The bartender was cute and slim. She had a red tube top on, no bra, and her nipples were staring right at Don, but he kept his eyes fixed on hers as she looked up at him and poured a beer from the tap into a glass and handed it to the gentleman next to Don. The man handed her a twenty, took a sip from the fizzy amber liquid and walked away into the crowd.

"What can I get you, hon?" she said. Her eyebrows raised with surprise when she realized he wasn't staring at her breasts. Next to the register, at the corner of the bar, was a chalk board with specials written in white chalk. The mirror behind her stretched behind the bar and a wall with red lights outlined the shelf of liquor bottles. There were an impressive ten different beer taps that ranged from domestic light beers to IPA craft beers from breweries all over the world.

"Hon? I could be your father."

"Hey, buddy. To each his own. If that's the way you like it." She snapped her gum as she showed her pearlescent whites to Don, with a simultaneous wink.

Don chuckled. "I'll take a bourbon on the rocks." He gleamed back at her.

"Oh. You like it hard, huh?" She pulled a glass out from under the shelf, scooped ice into it and poured the bourbon into the short glass till it hit the rim without spilling a drop.

"Are you normally this upfront with your customers? Or am I the lucky one?"

"I just like a real man when I see one." His eyes locked with hers for a moment. He paused, her toned abs and gold belly button ring glaring in Don's peripherals. She had to be about half his age. She couldn't be more than 26, and he was rounding 50.

"What's your name, kiddo?" Don tipped the brim of his hat up.

"Betty," she said, taking a rag and wiping down the countertop in front of Don.

"Nice to meet you, Betty. I'm Don." Don reached his hand out over the bar.

"Nice to meet you, Don." Betty shook Don's hand and showed her whites again. Betty's dimples grew on Don, the longer he stared at them, the cuter they became. The little buttons reminded him of his niece when she was a little girl, which made her about the same age as Betty.

"Listen, Betty. I think you're a really pretty girl, but you're too young for me."

"Ah, it was worth a try." She frowned and continued to clean some glasses with the white terry cloth.

"How much do I owe you?" Don reached into his back pocket.

"Don't worry. This one is on the house." She held her hands up, waving them back and forth.

"You don't have to do that." Don held out a twenty-dollar bill.

"No, it's fine. It's the best I can do for hitting on you so hard." They both cracked a smile and let out a small giggle.

"Listen, I have something to ask you." Don clasped onto his glass.

"Shoot." Betty leaned over the bar and propped herself onto her crossed forearms, cocking one ear forward to hear over the music.

"How long have you been working in this bar?"

"About fifteen months now. Give or take a month or two."

"How many girls have you seen come in here that have been underage, you think?"

"Hey, I don't serve to minors if that's what you're asking." Betty said, clearly offended.

"No. No. Just wondering. You know about the missing girls around here, right?"

"Yeah, that is a shame. I feel so bad. I wish there was something I could do.

"Well maybe there is."

"Like what?"

Another man stepped up to the bar next to Don, graying hair, short and straight with a light beard to match, lines written across his forehead that placed him at about the same age as Don. He glanced over at Don while taking a seat and proceeding to stare at Betty. His eyes diverted right to her breasts and she saw him staring at them.

"Hey, Gerry. Eyes up here," she said clearly irritated.

"You shouldn't wear something so revealing then." He was a regular at the bar and had a little zest in him that showed he didn't care much what people thought of him. He wore a Ramones t-shirt, and dark jeans with black work boots.

"You know it gets hot in here when it's crowded."

"Oh, I know. That's why I swing by on your busy nights. For the free show."

"Rude!" Betty was riddled with disgust.

"I would like a gin and tonic, please." He licked his lips and placed his hands on the bar counter, knocking his knuckles on the granite like he had a twitch he needed to fix. He was impatiently looking around, scoping out the room.

"Got it." Betty turned around and began making his drink. She poured gin and filled the glass with tonic water from the soda gun while Gerry spied on the room behind him. The jukebox, in the corner of the bar, lit up all different colors. It wasn't like a juke box from years ago with records or even CD's in it. The digital music player recalled a song at a moment's notice, and for only a dollar-fifty, you could pick any track to hear, from AC/DC to Justin Timberlake. Don followed his glances to the hipster kids at the box, faces lit up blue and red, picking out some newer music that Don never heard before. It was something the kids today heard from social media more than likely. MTV was something of the past, now it was all about Apple Music, and what you had in your playlist. This generation confused him, but as much as he was flabbergasted by the ingenious internet junkies of today, Don knew they still needed protecting from the evil of the world. Especially these young girls that had no idea what this world could do to them.

Betty put down the glass in front of Gerry. Don continued studying Gerry while he took a sip from his full glass, clicking his tongue against his teeth and making a sour face.

"Nice to see someone else here my age." Gerry turned to him with an odd look on his face, almost like he was annoyed at the gesture.

"Well, a man's gotta drink, even when there's a bunch of hoodlums running about," he said straight-faced. Then he laughed.

Don looked confused for a moment, looking into Gerry's gray eyes and chuckled.

"What brings you here?" Don asked, sipping his bourbon.

"Oh, I just enjoy getting out of the house from time to time."

"You live in town?"

"Yeah. Right up Pinecrest and 5th avenue."

"You walk here?"

"I did, but sometimes I take my truck when I get off work late. I'm a one and done kind of guy."

"I wish I had your strength."

"I don't keep any booze at the house because it would be the end of me. If I have one and go home, I have nothing else to drink. I guess it takes some courage, but it is what I have gotten used to."

"So why this bar? Why not the one on Twin Lakes drive? That usually has more adults more our age."

"I could ask you the same question." Gerry took another sip of his drink while shooting his brows higher.

"I suppose you could." Don held out his drink and raised his eyebrow, waiting for an answer.

"I guess you could say I like to keep up with the youth of today. I like to see what kind of trouble they're getting into."

"Trouble?" Don squinted.

"It's like the same trouble you and I got into at their ages. Intermingling with people they just met, making bad decisions based on liquid courage."

"Oh, I see."

"The fact of the matter is, some of them make it home, and some of them don't."

"What do you mean?" Don peered into Gerry's eyes as he sipped the gin and tonic.

"I would imagine I don't have to spell it out for you..." Gerry stopped, waiting for Don's unequivocal introduction.

"Oh, I'm Don." Placing his drink down on the coaster, Don extended his hand to Gerry.

"Gerald. Most people call me Gerry." They shook hands. "Nice to meet you, Don."

"Same here, Gerry." Don picked up his drink and circled the melting ice in the bourbon, faintly making a clinking sound against the glass. Don extended his drink towards Gerry and they touched glasses. "Cheers." Don swigged the last gulp and set the glass on the coaster of the granite surface. Gerry took a mild sip and turned his head toward the back of the bar.

"What did you mean about the kids not getting home?" Don pursed his lips, his face tilted to one side inquisitively. Gerry chuckled to himself which put Don at unease.

"Let me explain. Some of them end up in another person's house, or they try to make it on their own and are too inebriated to get there." Gerry looked at Don slyly. "Was that what you had in mind?"

"I guess the drink made me think something else." Don blankly stared at Gerry.

"I can remember when I was about their ages, hanging out in this bar with some buddies of mine, three sheets to the wind. We used to pick up women all the time. Brings back memories, you know?"

"Yeah, there was a time." Don closed his eyes for a moment and struggled to reopen them.

"Are you ok?" Gerry asked, waking Don from his fading mind.

"Long day, I guess. I should get home." Don got up from the barstool and leaned over the bar where Betty had been at the opposite end serving some patrons.

"Thanks again, Betty," he called out with his hand cupped against his mouth, putting the other hand in the air.

"You got it. Don't be a stranger now, you hear," Betty called back at him. Don winked and pulled a 20-dollar bill out of his pocket and stuffed it in the tip jar once she turned her back to him.

"That's mighty nice of you," Gerry said, then sipped his gin.

"Yeah well, she's a mighty nice girl," Don sarcastically said back, slightly slurring his words.

"How much did you have to drink, Don?" Gerry asked, looking up at him.

"Just one. I'm a one and done-er just like you now." He winked at Gerry. "I guess I didn't eat anything earlier, so it hit me a little harder than normal. I'll be alright, just got to get some food in me." Don patted his belly and then rubbed it in quick concentric circles.

"There's a place up the block. The Twin Lakes Diner serves till 3am. You should get something to eat there. Best eggs in the state."

"Thanks, I'll do that." Don turned around made his way towards the door. He felt the effects of the bourbon coursing his veins.: the warm feeling in his belly, his legs felt like rubber, his body slightly swaying as he walked towards the door. Some intense techno music came on, the bass rattled the walls, blaring noises of a synthesizer whining, and he plugged his ears with his fingers. Each beat thumped at his shoulders like someone was trying to push him over.

Young folks danced with drinks in their hands, hooting and hollering in a drunken manner. He eyed a couple on the dance floor not thirty feet from the bar, close to each other, touching and grazing like he hadn't seen before. Their perfect skin, and toned bodies made him feel self-conscious. His belly had been expanding these days and his face felt saggy—heavier than it did years before.

Don watched a young man with his hair slicked back grope a young lady with a blonde ponytail. He was squeezing her butt and breasts in front of everyone, but no one seemed to be watching except for Don. The young man grabbed at her ferociously and she seemed to enjoy every second of it. His eyes dried from staring and he had to blink, rubbing his eyes in disbelief at what went on. *Oh, to be young again.* He shook his head of perverted, sexual thoughts and regained consciousness of the reason he was here in the first place.

Don wasn't keen to the new world of the younger genera-tion. He tried to stay out of it as much as possible. Most of the music he heard by this generation sounded like noise to him. Don just wanted to pop on a Jimi Hendrix record and show these kids what real music was. But he knew they wouldn't care—in fact, they might beat the shit out of him for ruin-ing their sexual experiences. If there was one thing that lived through the 60's, 70's, and the 80's, it was free love, kids just called it hooking up today. Nothing wrong with having a little fun, but there was a thin line that could be easily crossed when fun turned into rape—possibly even murder given certain cir-cumstances.

Don's eyes speared like arrows at the young fellow. Maybe someone like him could be murdering these girls. Don walked over to the slick haired kid while he was mid-dance with the blonde girl, pulling his arm backward. Don forced slick back a couple feet like he was pulling a bad kid off the playground by his wrist for bad behavior.

"Get your hands off her," Don barked into Slick's face. Slick cocked his head toward Don.

"What the fuck, old man?" Slick's eyes lit up with surprise, with a sense of irritation.

"Don't touch him you creep!" the young girl said. Her face filled with fury. Her blonde ponytail swayed while she rocked back and forth from one leg to the other.

"What do you think you're doing to her?" Don angrily spat into Slick's face.

"We're just having fun, man. This is my girlfriend."

"If you don't let go of him now, I'm calling the police, but after I kick your ass." Blondie shouted at Don. Her young, unwrinkled face contorted with the attempts to keep a raging beast from jumping out.

"I would listen to her, dude. She's a blackbelt."

"Yeah, sure." Don puffed out air in disbelief.

Within a second, Blondie had reached over to Don, used the lapel of his jacket to pull him toward her, and then dropped him to the floor by sweeping out his legs from under him in one swift move. A giant thud catapulted across the room that could be heard over the music. Everyone in the bar stopped what they were doing and looked at Don sprawled out on his back on the hard wood floor.

"Next one will put you in the hospital for sure," Blondie said, walking away with Slick's hand in hers.

"Are you alright, Don?" Betty called out to Don from behind the bar. Don gasped for air, coughing from the air being pummeled out of him. With his first long breath he gargled out, "Yeah."

Gerry held his hand out and pulled Don up to his feet. Don brushed himself off and looked behind him where the two kids had been making out with each other on the dance floor.

"Let's get out of here," Gerry said and helped him out the door. The music continued, and the kids cheered as Don exited the bar.

Don's arm straddled over Gerry's neck, moving at a slow pace out the doors of the bar and to the parking lot lit by the pink fluorescent glow of the bar sign.

"That's fine. Right here is good," Don said, straightening himself and kinking his neck, wincing in pain.

"What the hell was that?" Gerry said concernedly.

"Nothing. Just thought he was doing something he shouldn't be doing to that girl."

"Ah, I see."

"With all these girls going missing, it felt like I was doing a duty that needed to be done. You never know," Don said, stepping into the parking lot. The dirt covered gravel reached about fifty yards to the street that continued down to the lakes. The parking lot was full, all sorts of cars and trucks piled into small slotted spots with faded yellow lines.

"Are you the police or something?" Gerry twisted at the facial hair on his chin.

"Uh...No...No...Just a concerned citizen that's all." Don straightened his hat on his head.

"Well you definitely made quite an ass of yourself in there."

"Yeah, I guess I did, didn't I?" Don rubbed his neck. He could still hear the thumping of the bass coming from inside the bar. "I guess I can't show my face in there anymore after that escapade."

"I would say not until spring break is over. These kids will be gone next week."

"Yeah, that's true."

"How are you feeling?"

"I think I need to get to that diner."

"How about I go with you?"

Don scratched the back of his head and thought for a minute.

"Yeah, that's fine. I could use some company." They walked down the street, the overhead lamps buzzing as they passed underneath them. A cool breeze blew through the old banyan trees, their roots falling from branches, forming separate trunks of trees that marked a century or more. People had come and gone while these trees grew bigger and fatter, preserved by the same people in this town that kept secrets and committed murders. The thought of Cynthia's killer still at large made Don sick to his stomach and it wasn't the drinking, it was the thought of finding another girl on the lakeshore.

Don closed his eyes and saw Cynthia's face. He could see how cold and blue she was. She had a look to her, peacefully in slumber like Sleeping Beauty, but never to wake again. He followed her eyebrows to the bridge of her nose, her purple lips—moist and red only 12 hours ago. He stood directly over her now, the blue haze that filled the air on the sandy shore of the lake. Her eyelids opened and black glassy balls looked back at him, so black he could see himself in the reflection. Cynthia's eyes fluttered. Simultaneously voices conjured in his head, like a multitude of whispers caught in his ears all at once. *Save me,* he heard over, and over again. How could he save her, she was already dead?

He woke from his trance while walking down the street with Gerry. They were up the street from the diner now, and right by the east lake. Don couldn't remember the last five to ten minutes. He knew he just walked over a half mile, with Gerry, but didn't know how they got there. It was like time fast forwarded and he had no recollection of the walk, other than seeing Cynthia's body.

Autumn's dried leaves ruffled across the street from a gust of wind. The awkward silence grew between them until Don said something. Cars whizzed by and honked in the distance. The interstate led directly to Twin Lakes to bring business to the town especially during this time of season: people that had expendable income, kids from college, rich investors, business owners, anyone looking to get away and have a good time on the waterfront. Money was spent on food and unnecessary items. Memorabilia for their visit to town usually consisted of clothes, art, and smoke shop paraphernalia.

Don was growing impatient, waiting for that phone call from forensics about the DNA test results. Would he be so lucky to find someone that left there shit behind on accident, or on purpose to give him the run around? *What was the answer?* Don perused through his mind. Drinking on an empty stomach didn't help either. He felt sick and dizzy to the point of an unforgiving headache.

"You don't look so good, Don," Gerry said, placing his hand on Don's slumped shoulder.

"I'm alright. Just hungry." Don's lips were dry, and his face was pale.

"So, what do you do by the way?" Gerry said.

"I'm a det..." Don coughed and cleared his throat. "I'm a dentist."

"Oh, I probably shouldn't tell you that I have like fifteen cavities then."

"Probably not. I may think you're a bad person." Don snickered.

"I just can't stop eating those sweets, doc," Gerry said to Don sarcastically.

"That's ok, I have a hard time with them too."

"Really? I didn't think dentists ever ate candy."

"I do. I just brush my teeth right afterward."

"Yeah, I don't do that."

"Well, there is your problem. What about you? What do you do?"

"Construction," Gerry said. "I run Twin Lakes Construction."

"You own the company?"

"Yeah, sorta. I have a couple partners and we split the duties and all."

"Wow, I didn't know I was amongst a famous person here."

"Yeah, well, not a big deal really."

"Your family is one of the founding families in this area, and you have built most of the homes on the east side of the lake, isn't that right?"

"Yeah, but not a big deal really. I'm just a guy, just like you."

"Sorry, I didn't mean to get all excited. It's not every day you get to walk down the street with a prominent figure in the community."

"It's nothing really." Gerry put his hand on Don's shoulder and gave it a squeeze. Don looked at Gerry's hand and noticed some scratches that looked like fingernail marks.

"What happened there?"

"Oh, just something while I was on the job. From time to time I get scratched by something. We wear the hard hats, so we don't get hit in the head with anything, but I never wear my gloves when I'm on site." Don nodded his head. His phone buzzed in his pocket. It was Chad calling from the lab. The vibration continued.

"Hold on one second, I need to take this." Don walked away from Gerry, about fifteen feet away from a streetlight they stopped under.

"Anything yet?" He asked Chad, cupping his mouth with his hand around the bottom of his phone.

"No. No matches yet. It's been going through the database for a couple hours now." Chad said while chewing on the other side of the phone.

"Did you have to call me while you were eating?"

"I just took a bite of some liquorice."

"While you're with the body?"

"Not like she's hungry."

"Just do me a favor. Look under the girl's fingernails, see what you can find there. Any dead skin she may have ripped off from the killer." Don grumbled with hints of aggravation.

"You got it." Chad continued to chew.

"Stop chewing in my ear."

"Sorry." The chewing stopped. Don felt bad.

"I got a headache. Sorry I yelled at you."

"It's ok. Where are you now?"

"Just get it done and call me back when you got something."

"OK..." Don hung up the phone and walked back over to Gerry.

"Everything alright?"

"Yeah, all good."

It was 1:35am by the time they got in the place, sat down, ordered with Kasey, the waitress, and started eating. The place smelled of a lemon scented cleansing agent, and freshly baked cherry pie. It was a clean diner. All the tables were wiped down, the floors waxed and buffed, freshly mopped before they arrived. The classic black and white checkered tile floors, rounded tables with chrome siding, and red leather seats pulled the style of the fifties into 2019. The old cars and movie stars hung from the walls, slightly faded from the sun. Old '57 Chevys, and Marilyn Monroe seemed to blend together like cake and ice cream.

Don held a fat burger in his hand and took a sloppy bite of the beastly sandwich. Burger juice and ketchup with shreds of lettuce fell onto the fresh potato wedges. Don knew this wasn't the best meal choice, but he was starving and knew it would help his headache go away—although his stomach would be cursing him later for eating such greasy foods.

"This is more like my kind of place," Don said with his mouth full, wiping ketchup from his lips with a napkin he pulled from the chrome dispenser.

"Yeah, I agree. Maybe we're too old for the bars now." Gerry forked a piece of cherry pie into his mouth. Kasey came back with refills for the guys. She poured coffee into their ceramic mugs, resting on saucers. She wore a black uniform with a white collar, a name tag in red letters on a white background pinned to her lapel. The pouch of her black apron held her notepad and spare change. Kasey's shiny red shoes reminded Don of Dorothy in the Wizard of Oz. Her brown hair was pulled back behind her ears into a bun, and her blue eyes glistened when she spoke.

"Can I get you guys anything else?" she said. Her lips matched her shoes.

"No thanks, Kasey. You've been a delight." Don tipped his hat at the young woman.

"Thank you, sir." Kasey pulled out her order pad and wrote the total down and slid it on the table. "Take your time, fellas. No rush."

"Thanks, Kasey." She walked away and headed behind the counter to the kitchen. There were three other tables with people sitting at them. She was the only one working tonight with the cook in the back.

"I got it." Don grabbed the check before Gerry could get to it.

"Let me."

"I insist. You helped me out back there. I appreciate it. I may not have made it here tonight if it weren't for you."

"Let me at least pay for my half."

"No. Your money is no good here."

"Thank you," Gerry said and forked the last sliver of pie into his mouth. "I really do enjoy a piece of pie." He picked up the napkin off his lap and wiped his mouth.

"Make sure you brush your teeth when you get home." Don laughed, pretending he was letting out some dentist humor.

"That's a good one." Gerry chuckled.

DON AND GERRY EXITED the diner and were walking down the cement steps when Don's phone vibrated. He knew it was Chad. Don waited until they were clear of the steps before he answered the call.

"Hold on a second." Don pulled his phone from his pocket again and signaled with his index finger to Gerry.

"Who calls you at two in the morning?" Gerry asked, surprised.

"My wife, making sure I'm ok. I normally don't stay out this late." Don walked off and answered the phone.

"So, I got a match. There was a glitch in the system, and it froze for a bit, but I got it to work…"

"Just tell me who it is!"

"Well. That's the thing. There are two different pieces of DNA here."

"So, what's the secret? Give me the news already."

"Ok, well this one is a doozy because the first match of DNA I got was from a record originally deleted from the databases. So, I had to physically dig it out of the files in the warehouse. He was originally arrested for raping and molesting a girl back in 85 but the charges were dropped afterwards. Doesn't say why."

"Who was on the case?"

"Well that's the thing…" Chad paused and breathed heavily over the phone—the keyboard pitter-pattered in the background.

"What do you mean?"

"Deputy Michael Holden was on the case in 1985. Well, Sheriff Holden now. And here's the kicker. He was the other piece of DNA under Cynthia's fingernails."

"What? Really?"

"That's what it says here."

Don wondered why Mike never mention anything about a rape case he was involved with as a deputy. Don had known Mike since before they were in the academy together. Why would he bury this evidence, and not tell him? None of this was making any sense to Don.

"Have you told anyone yet?"

"No. You're my first call."

"Who's the sperm guy?" He held the phone close to his mouth and whispered so Gerry couldn't hear him.

"Oh yeah. A Mr. Gerald Hays, I cross referenced the name and found this guy is part of one of the founding families down here. He owns his own construction company here in town." So that was why Mike was hiding information. One of the founding families of Twin Lakes didn't want their boy going to jail for raping a young woman.

A sheriff cruiser rolled up outside the diner with flashing lights. Mike stepped out of the vehicle.

"Oh my God. I gotta go."

"Wait? What…" Don hung up the phone and slid it back into his pocket.

"Hey, Don," Mike called out, walking over with his thumbs hooked into his uniform's belt loops.

"How did you find me?"

"Your phone has a tracker, silly. For a detective you ain't too bright."

"Who's this guy, Don?" Gerry asked.

"You can cut the shit, Gerald. He knows already."

"How?"

"My wife told me."

"His better half indeed. The forensic scientist found our DNA."

"I thought you said she was clean."

"Well, if you didn't leave your scumbag behind, maybe this wouldn't have happened. I'm always cleaning up after you royals around here."

"We pay you enough."

"Hardly." The three stood there in a sort of semi-circle outside the diner. Some people in the diner looked out the window to see what was going on.

"Why, Mike? Being Sheriff wasn't enough for you?"

"Listen, I would love to explain this to you, but it looks like we have a crowd. What's going to happen now is you're going to get in my vehicle and we're going to take a little ride where we can talk this over like adults."

"Over my dead body."

"Don't make this harder than it has to be, Donnie boy." Mike pulled his hand from his belt loop and inched it toward his gun holstered on the side of his pants. Don looked back at the people looking through the windows. The waitress and the cook standing right next to each other, both perplexed. This was the most action this diner had ever seen before, so they were coming up with a thousand different scenarios right now in their minds.

"Donnie. I will shoot you in front of all these people. Tell them you were the serial killer, and we found you. Now put your gun on the ground and walk toward me."

Don slowly put his hands in the air and reached toward the back of his pants where his gun was concealed. He pulled it out by the butt with his fingers, the barrel of the gun facing down. He placed it on the ground and kicked it toward Gerry.

"Pick it up, Gerry," Mike said. Gerry walked over and grabbed the gun and handed it to Mike. "Alright, Donnie boy. You know what to do." Don walked toward the cruiser with his hands above his head. He looked at Mike the entire time, sneering at him with a victorious look. Don placed his hands on the hood on the vehicle followed by Mike slamming Don's head onto the hood of the cruiser and cuffing his hands behind his back without a struggle. Mike walked Don to the back of the cruiser, opened the door, and hit Don over the head with the butt of his gun, knocking him out.

THE MONOTONE PUFFY clouds were mirrored in the lake's glassy reflections. The water reached up the shoreline toward Don's naked toes as a young boy. The sand squished between his toes like soft mushy dough. He stared at a young girl's body on the shore, surrounded by adults trying to resuscitate her, but her lifeless body wouldn't give back to the countless repetitive compressions of C.P.R by a man wearing a silver bathing suit with two parallel stripes on the side.

Don stepped closer to her—his footprints cemented in the sand just inches apart. The closer he got, the faster his heart thumped. Everything was black and white and gray. Stepping closer he leaned over the crowd of people hovering over her body. Don stretched his neck and saw the poor dead girl's face. Her polka dot bathing suit, her straight as a needle lips, the subtle look of peace like a princess in slumber. Don studied her from head to toe, she changed slightly, her face conforming to Cynthia's face. The polka dot bathing suit transformed to jeans and a V-neck t-shirt. He turned around to shout for help, but the beach was empty. Don stood there as an adult, watching Cynthia awake, reaching her once limp, water-logged arms upward, hoisting herself upward onto her weakened legs. Cynthia stood up and dusted the sand off her back. Her young, dead face pointed at his. No words or sound could be heard. Silence graced his ears. The absence of wind rustling through the leaves, the chirps of birds were gone. Images faded into nothingness where darkness crept in. Cynthia swept away like sand in a desert storm. Sudden brightness flushed his vision. Slaps to his face awoke him. He squinted and adjusted to the light. His face felt numb, but the back of his head was throbbing. It felt wet on the surface as a breeze drifted over the open wound.

"Wake up," Gerry said. Don's head jerked with the motion of Gerry's hand struck his face once more. Don opened his eyes wider to see the headlights of the sheriff's cruiser pointed directly at him while he sat on the ground up against a tree somewhere in the forest. The sound of cicadas singing, and crickets chirping filtered through the dark forest.

"What's going on?" Don asked, finding some saliva to moisten his vocal cords.

"Well, Donnie boy, I guess I'm gonna have to tell you." Mike brought out Chad and threw him to the ground with a thump. Chad moaned with his hands tied behind his back.

"Why are you doing this?" Don asked. He shuffled his feet in the dirt to prop up his slumped spine. Gerry stood over Chad with Don's gun pointed at his head.

"Listen. I get why I'm here but let the kid go."

"No can-do, Donnie boy. He knows too much. All your fault," Mike said and turned his back to Don. He reached in the car to plant a cigarette in his mouth and lit it, tossing the lighter back onto the seat.

"See, unfortunately, I found the Twin Lakes killers here on patrol by myself and it so happened to be two people that worked in my department. With the planting of some evidence and an apologetic statement for hiring such incompetent men, I developed a hunch that led me to you here with this girl here."

Mike pointed over Don's shoulder to a hole dugout a couple of feet with a freshly killed young woman in her early twenties at most. Her dark brown hair tossed around in the dirt—her eyelids still open, staring blankly. The look of surprise frozen on her face and a blood soaked, white blouse.

"So obviously you know what happens here," Mike said.

"I thought you were better than this." Don's eyelids fluttered with anger. Mike nonchalantly nodded at Gerry standing next to Chad. He pushed the barrel of the nine-millimeter to Chad's skull, metal dug into his scalp, buried in the quaff of hair on his head.

"You don't have to do this, Gerry," Don said, pleading with the sadistic look on Gerry's face.

"Please don't kill me. I won't tell anyone I swear. I'll hide all the files. I'll burn them, get rid of the digital evidence. I can be a major asset to your operation. I'll work for free." The words and phrases strung together like he had been speaking gibberish. Gerry perplexingly looked at Mike for an answer.

"Not a bad idea," he said, holding his chin as he gave it some thought. "No." He winked at Gerry. The gun fired and Chad's brain splattered across at Don. He flinched as the blood sprayed his face and then he watched Chad's body hit the ground one last time for good.

"You sick fucks!" Don screamed out. He foamed from the mouth and wiped the blood splatter from his face with the sides of his shoulder.

"Sorry, Donny boy, this was the only way that this would work out," Mike said in between a chuckle. "You understand this is all part of my plan. The kid did have a pretty good offer though. I already destroyed all the evidence, so no need for that punk."

Mike strut over to Don holding his colt .45 in his hand. His uniform had some of Chad's blood on it.

"How are you going to explain the blood on your uniform?"

"I'm sure I can come up with something."

"Who's going to believe this massive lie you're telling anyway?" Don looked up at Mike staring back down at him. "The F.B.I will get involved soon as you bring my body in. They will ask you questions you probably haven't even thought of answering yet."

"What are you thinking, huh? That you're going to sway my decision to kill you right here?" Mike pointed the gun into Don's face. "Once I tell everyone that you were the killer and the evidence is there to back it up there isn't any questions to ask. Case Closed."

Don shifted his eyes to Gerry standing over Chad's body, gun pointed at the ground.

"What are you looking at, asshole?" Gerry said.

"You must be pretty sick, the only way a grade-A douche bag like you can sleep with younger women is to rape and kill them."

"Fuck you!" Gerry shuffled forward.

"That's enough." Mike cocked his head looking back at Gerry, who stopped dead in his tracks. The gun aimed in Don's face angled just enough to inch past his skull. Don lunged forward knocking the gun downward, the sudden movement inched the trigger firing a bullet to the ground before it fell out of his hand. Don knocked Mike backward, his body falling to his head aligned with Chad's blown open skull. Mike looked up at Gerry stiffly standing there with a surprised look on his face, as if he was frozen.

"Shoot him, you fuckin' idiot!" Gerry pulled his gun up to aim at Don scrambling with his handcuffs on his wrists. Don grabbed the gun on the ground and rolled to the side like a gator in a death roll, firing three shots at Gerry before he could get a shot at Don. Gerry's face went blank and a tear dropped from his eye as he looked down at the whole in his chest, blood leaking out. He touched it and held his hand in front of his face before he fell backwards, dropping the gun to his side as he fell. Now three bodies laid in a line on the ground. Mike saw the gun lying in the dirt and slowly raised himself to his palms. He propped himself up on his arms and lifted his upper torso to sit on the ground only inches from the gun. Don had Mike locked in his sights.

"Now, Don, let's not do anything rash," Mike said. Sweat gathered on his forehead.

"Did you plan this?" Don looked over at Gerry's body. Mike nervously angled his head over his shoulder and kept Don in his peripherals.

"I'm sure we can work something out."

"How do you plan on doing that?" Don said, breathing heavily. "Your cash cow is dead. It's over, Mike."

"Nothing's over till I say it's over." Mike reached for the gun and Don fired one last time, shooting Mike right in the side of the skull. The gun Mike reached for flew a couple feet from his body as the strike of the bullet flung his body sideways. The gun landed by the door of the cruiser. Don laid there for a moment and caught his breath, cocking his head like his neck was on a swivel. He gazed at each body cramped in such a small vicinity amongst the vast forest. Don put the gun down and sat up. Slowly, he raised up to his knees and then to his feet, completely exhausted and emotionally spent. He crept towards Mike's body, reached into his pocket, and grabbed the keys to the cuffs around his wrists. Sliding the key into the hole, Don popped off one cuff at a time and dropped them to the ground.

The booming sounds of the gun echoed across the lakes where Theodore Hutchinson had been on his porch looking across the lake. He was a retired machinist that was a light sleeper. The first shot woke him, so naturally he went outside in his robe to see if he would hear another shot. Theodore's lack of sleep made him think he was dreaming he had heard a gun, but when he heard three consecutive shots call across the lake while he stood on the back porch, he pulled his phone from his robe pocket, flipped it open and dialed 911.

Don grabbed the pack of cigarettes on the driver's seat before he plopped his butt down in the cruiser. He paused for a moment when he heard sirens faintly wailing in the distance. The sound of a helicopter whirled miles from the lakes. He smiled and tapped the radio knob and tuned the dial to a classic rock station that played Black Dog by Led Zeppelin. Don cranked the knob to full volume, the music echoing through the forest. He popped a cigarette into his mouth and grabbed the clear, red plastic, Bic lighter from the seat. He flicked the flint and cupped the flame in the palm of his hand over the tip of the cigarette. The ember burned bright as he inhaled the nicotine from the tobacco, filling his lungs with smoke and blowing it out effortlessly. nodding to beat of the song. Don looked at the old banyan tree through the windshield. The rooted piece of history stood there in its magnificent formation, glowing from the headlights shining up its bark into the hanging branches. The banyan tree that started as a seedling sprung amongst the sea of elder trees, experiencing the life of the world that grazed upon its plentiful forest, watching things live and die on the grounds of Twin Lakes. Don inhaled deeply, sucking the life from the cigarette, the end burning bright red. Don tapped the steering wheel with his fingers and exhaled a plume of smoke.

Day-Break Trailer Park

The sun rose like it did every day onto the close knit, aluminum sided, black and brown roofs of the Daybreak Members Community Trailer Park.

Samuel Guston relaxed inside his screened in porch like he did every morning, afternoon, and night. He considered himself the watch dog of the community. He had retired ten years ago as a security guard and settled into this community to find peace and quiet among the other folks with the same idea. Samuel enjoyed watching the birds perch on the limbs of nearby trees—the way their songs soothed his nerves while he filled his lungs with the humidity of the Florida air. He even enjoyed the rain after long, hot summer days—breathing in the sweet aroma of petrichor. This is what he lived for now. Relaxation and a stress-free environment without work to be done, or responsibilities.

There were two children that ran around the community destroying everything in their path and Samuel did not tolerate his peace and quiet being disturbed by these whippersnappers. One block over from Samuel's was a single mother with two boys, a year apart. Since neither one of their father's carried any responsibility towards them, their mother had to work endlessly to make ends meet just to keep a roof over their head and food on the table. Samuel knew the dilemma that the boys had gone through and knew that their mother, Kacey, did not deserve the hand she had been dealt. Unfortunately for her, while she was working, these boys wreaked havoc upon the park, disturbing the peace and causing a ruckus all hours of the day. Jaden and Hayden would torment the streets on garbage day, knocking over the cans that held putrid smelling waste. The boys would always seem to tip the cans over on garbage day right before the truck would pick them up. The rotting smell would sour the day for Samuel and the other residents that had an olfactory system left. The garbage truck passed by all the cans that were overturned into the streets, sometimes running over the remnants and plastering the contents to the hot pavement. Jaden and Hayden found this particularly funny because they only did half the job to make a bigger mess than intended. Even knowing that these boys had no role model to look up to, and family problems he couldn't fathom at this age in his life, Samuel still wanted to beat these boys to teach them a lesson like he had learned when he was a young lad.

Samuel's old, wooden rocking chair squeaked with momentum as he enjoyed a blissful summer morning. He saw those little brats push over his garbage can from his porch—the contents spilled into the street right in front of his trailer. One of the bags broke open and the wind carried some loose papers and cellophane down the street. The foul-smelling juices leaked out and created a thick, sticky layer on top of the pavement. Samuel knew the putrid smell would last until the rain would wash it away. Ultimately, Samuel had to clean up after the mess. It took the park weeks to pick up floating trash around the community, and once they had it clean again, the boys would dump more cans and the same problem would arise.

Samuel watched the boys flee down the block like they were running from the cops.

"You little shits! Come back here and clean this up!" Samuel sprung from his chair and shouted down the street.

"Go fuck yourself, old man," one of them would say. Followed by, "Eat my shit, slow poke." They cackled, running as fast as they could, Samuel with his bum knee could never catch them, even when he tried to surprise them waiting behind a tree just before they tipped the can. They always seemed to slip from his grasp like little, slimy eels.

"I'll catch you one day," Samuel always muttered to himself. Samuel enjoyed this park so much, but he wished there was something he could do about these two little bastards that seemed to think they ran it.

After numerous combative conversations with their mother, Samuel knew that wasn't going to solve the problem. The cops couldn't do anything because they had bigger fish to fry. Jaden and Hayden were too young to go to jail for such petty crimes. Samuel was mostly worried for the boys' well-being. If they didn't learn their lesson early on in life, maybe they would be spending their lives in jail one day. That was no way for them to grow up, obviously Kacey didn't care, or she didn't have time to care—working twelve-hour shifts at the diner downtown.

After a while Samuel began to feel like Mr. Wilson in Dennis the Menace, except there were not one but two menaces, and at least Dennis' parents were nice. Mr. Wilson didn't know how well he had it.

One-night Samuel was enjoying the evening after devouring a beautiful, cooked steak he had prepared for his wife, Bernadette, and himself. Jaden and Hayden ran up to Samuel's house and threw ten eggs at his front porch, blasting the gooey, yellow yolk all over the blue aluminum siding and on the front door he painted white just the weekend before.

Samuel busted out the front door like a bull through the gates at a rodeo, but the boys were already halfway down the street shouting back at Samuel, "Fart faced fuck."

Samuel was so heated he felt like if no one was going to do something he would do it. He contemplated taking the broom handle and beating their bottoms until they were red. Or taking his belt and whacking the two of their asses as hard as he could. As those thoughts ran through his mind, he realized he didn't want to spend the rest of his days of retirement in jail either, so he cooled down and washed the eggs off his house while muttering under his breath.

"Stop muttering to yourself, Sammy, sounds like you're insane," Bernadette called out from inside the house. "I'll show you insane, woman," Samuel murmured.

"What was that?"

"Nothing, dear. Be right there." It was amazing what the old bat could hear sometimes. She couldn't hear two kids blasting the house with eggs, but she could hear the whispers of an old man disrespecting his wife behind her back.

Samuel thought of all the times Jaden and Hayden made his life a living hell. He felt like there was more work with these two delinquents around than the thirty years as a security guard dealing with drunks and entitled dickheads. He remembered the time he had to replace his mailbox because the boys whacked it off with a baseball bat, screaming "Bald fuck!" while running down the street.

Almost every Thursday they would drive by on their shitty bikes and throw their mom's empty beer bottles at Samuel while he was getting in his car. How badly he wanted to run those little shits over while they were out cruising, but he couldn't think of a way he could get away with vehicular manslaughter just because two pissheads threw bottles at him.

The Tampa police didn't give a crap about the trailer park. Half the times when they were called, they wouldn't even show up. Samuel thought he was a tax paying citizen just like everyone else, but he guessed if those officers showed up for every garbage can overturned, egg thrown, glass bottle broken, and flaming bag of shit, they wouldn't be able to make a difference catching bad guys or writing tickets to people driving fifteen miles over the speed limit.

Bernadette got upset with Samuel. "They're just kids. It's a phase they will grow out of if you pay them no attention." Samuel found that funny because she was never the one to clean up their messes or be called degrading names by kids no older than the shit he took before he retired.

Samuel actually forgot about the little brats while he let the beautiful rays of sun blanket him in the small corner of his lot. The warmth of the sun soothed Samuel's skin from the outside in like a brownie fresh out of the oven. Samuel loved that toasty warm feeling—tiny beads of sweat gathered on his forehead while classic rock and roll played on the radio. This reminded him of a time he knew so well. A time when he fell in love with Bernadette on the dance floor to Hamilton, Joe Frank & Reynolds—*Fallin in Love*. As he enjoyed the moment, eyes closed, dreaming of his wife in her youth, Samuel was living in bliss until Jaden and Hayden dumped a pitcher of ice water over Samuel's head, dousing him from head to toe. He jumped out of the chair and had two fistfuls of shirts before the boys could finish laughing. He stared into their scared shitless faces with such intensity, something popped just as he was about to clock their heads together. The massive pain coursed his chest like he had never felt before. Samuel's grasp weakened. Jaden and Hayden's feet landed back on the ground. The boys ran out of Samuel's yard as fast as their twiggy legs could carry their heavy bodies. Samuel crumpled to his knees and Bernadette happened to look out the window as his body collided with the grass. She ran out of the house in her muumuu and shower cap, pulled Samuel by the shoulders, and rolled him onto his back. He looked up at Bernadette and saw her mouth moving but couldn't make out a word she said. The sun blinded him, so he closed his eyes and the next minute he knew, he was bouncing around on a stretcher headed into an ambulance with two young paramedics.

Samuel awoke in a hospital bed hooked to machines. He remembered the tremendous pain traveling though his chest like a cannonball had been thrown on top his rib cage. The weight crushed his thoughts and kept oxygen from filling his lungs. For a moment he forgot what put him in this hospital till he saw the faces of Jaden and Hayden walk through the door of his room alongside his wife, Bernadette.

"Are you trying to give me another heart attack, woman?"

"Go ahead, boys." Bernadette pushed the delinquents towards Samuel's bed by their shoulders. They wore fright on their faces while they mustered some words together, looking at each other, waiting for a cue.

"Jaden? Hayden? Do as we discussed now." Bernadette crossed her arms over her bosoms dressed in her finest Sunday clothes, an outfit Samuel hadn't seen his wife wear in ages.

"Yes, ma'am," the boys said in unison. "We're sorry, Mr. Guston, for giving you a heart attack."

"And?" Bernadette raised her eyebrows.

"We're going to clean your house," Jaden said.

"And we're going to take out your garbage every week," Hayden chimed in.

"No more causing mischief in the neighborhood?" Samuel looked over at Bernadette.

"Well no more mischief toward you, Sam."

"Is this true, boys?"

"Yes, sir."

"How did you get these kids to do this?" Samuel asked Bernadette.

"They need some direction, and I told them who to bother as long as it didn't involve you." Bernadette knew the boys had a rough upbringing. Without telling Samuel every detail while they were in the hospital room together, she had promised to help the boys with their homework and would provide a home cooked meal every week. She knew all they needed was guidance and love and they would turn their behavioral issues around.

"Who?" Sam asked.

A couple weeks after Samuel returned home from the hospital, he lounged outside in his chair under the sun once again. Jaden and Hayden had left Samuel alone just like they promised, and they had dinner every Tuesday night with Samuel and Bernadette. They cleaned up the house and repainted the front door they ruined with eggs. Samuel was proud of the boys for their accomplishments and almost forgot how bad they've been in the past.

Samuel was enjoying the warmth of the sun when he heard some crashing behind the trailer next door and heard his neighbor Frank yelling at Jaden and Hayden, giggling as they ran away.

"You sons of a bitch! Get back here and clean this up."

"Eat a dick!" Jaden yelled back.

Samuel smiled and thought, it's good to be back home.

Special Thanks

I would like to thank all the people that made this book possible, from the ones that inspired me to believe in myself, to the ones that helped me shape this body of work into what it is today.

Thanks to my family. My editor Katrina Roets. Rebecca Covers for my cover design.

These stories couldn't have been possible without the help from Erica Dawson, Lynn Bartis, Stefan Kiesbye, Jason Ockert, Kevin Moffitt, Don Morrill, Alan Michael Parker, Josip Novakovich, Jessica Anthony, Corinna Vallianatos, Roy Peter Clark, Sandra Beasley and all of the University of Tampa staff and faculty that helped put a wonderful program together, teaching, mentoring, and nurturing my writing skills.

To all the writers I met during the residencies, students, and professionals. You helped shape the craft of writing for me to complete this and embark on the journey of a writer.

Thank you to everyone and those I may not have mentioned. Know that you positively affected my life and I appreciate the lessons I've learned along the way.

About the Author

Sean **Malloy** is an American writer residing in the Tampa Bay area in Florida.

He received his Master of Fine Arts from the University of Tampa in 2018 and has continued to focus on writing as a profession. His working thesis "*Wings Upon Flames*" took shape in the final semester which became a finished body of work. Sean is in the process of working on his first novel and continues to inspire other writers through his advice and experience on his podcast he created for all writers of all stages in the craft called "Walking Writers Podcast."

Don't miss out!

Visit the website below and you can sign up to receive emails whenever Sean Malloy publishes a new book. There's no charge and no obligation.

https://books2read.com/r/B-A-FDVH-KKBY

BOOKS 2 READ

Connecting independent readers to independent writers.

Milton Keynes UK
Ingram Content Group UK Ltd.
UKHW010148191023
430900UK00005B/454

9 780578 678696